The Fate of the Stone

of the

Stone

Part 2

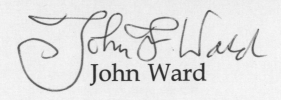

John Ward

The Stone of Sorrow

of

Sorrow

The Revealer of Wonders

Studio 9 Books

Ordering information:

United States(trade):
Koen Book Distributors
10 Twosome Drive, Moorestown, NJ 08057
☎ 856-235-4444
or Baker & Taylor

Canada:
Jaguar Book Group
100 Armstrong Ave., Georgetown, Ontario L7G 5S4
☎ 905-877-4483, 🖷 905-877-4410,
SAN: 118-8801
E-mail: sales@jaguarbookgroup.ca

or from the publisher (special & group orders):
Studio 9 Books Inc.
Plattsburgh, NY 12901 & Montreal, Canada H3H 1A7
☎ 514-934-5433 🖷 514-937-8765
e-mail: studio9@rdppub.com

United Kingdom and Europe (except France):
Booksource, 32 Finlas Street
Cowlairs Estate, Glasgow, G22 5DU
☎ 08702-402-182 (UK telephone) 44-141-558-1366 (international)
🖷 44-141-557-0189

France:
Casteilla, S.A.
10 rue Léon Foucault,
78180 Montigny-le-Bretonneux, France
☎ 01-30-14-19-30 🖷 01-30-14-19-46

We wish to thank the Sodec (Québec) for its generous support
of our publishing program in both French and English.

Printed in Canada

To my wife

From one century to another, follow The Stone of Sorrow and the lives of those who seek its power.

Two scenes from the past

I – Ferrara, December 1515

The scaffold stands at the open end of the square. It is not a gallows, for the one to die is no common criminal: it is merely a platform, a stepping stone to the true instrument of death, a towering stake made from the trunk of a single tree, thrusting skyward like a monstrous warning finger out of the mountainous pile of brushwood banked up around it.

It is a little after noon but the light is already failing on this short winter's day: the sky is heavy with the threat of snow. From the balconies of the houses that enclose the other three sides of the square limp banners hang, forlorn attempts to make a festival of the grisly spectacle to come. The balconies themselves are crowded with the well-to-do, the nobles and the magnates with their consorts (and their children – the sight of a man being burnt alive is held to be highly educational) all decked out in their finest raiment.

Their physical elevation, high above the crowd, is an expression of their social superiority – the square below is given over to the rabble, thronged in their thousands.

Some young men of quality, filled with youthful bravado, have abandoned the security of their houses to rough it with the mob: plentiful ducats dispensed in the right quarter have secured them a prime location at the very foot of the pyre, where they now stand, conspicuous in their sumptuous finery. None looks at ease, but four of them are making the best of it, exchanging banter in voices just a little too loud, with laughter a shade too hearty; only the fifth wears his distress openly on his handsome, sensitive face. Is it just the nearness of the stinking masses that disturbs him, or the prospect of what is to come? Certainly the pyre and the stake seem to hold him with a horrified fascination.

He is a tall youth, and sports a gorgeous bonnet of brilliant blue adorned with an egret's plume which makes him stand out like a beacon. All around him, a sea of murmuring voices discuss the man whose execution all have come to see:

– The Mage Albanus, says one. The greatest wizard of the age!

– It's said that in him the spirit of Michael Scot yet lives!

Several bless themselves at the mention of that fearful name: Michael Scot the sorcerer, three hundred years dead, lives on in popular repute.

– The greatest wizard of the age? scoffs another. Then tell me – why is he here? The man that overcame him now, that's the greater wizard, in my opinion!

– Ruggiero it was, pipes up an excitable little man,

Ruggiero of Montefeltro – my own part of the world, he adds, swelling with vicarious pride.

– As to that, says the first man vehemently, he was not overcome at all, but betrayed by one he trusted as his agent – this Ruggiero – a quacksalver mountebank posing as an Alchemist, a peddler of philtres and potions to lovesick girls and impotent old men, a posturing dolt, and no Italian either, but a two-faced, double-dealing Englishman!

– The English are all traitors, shrills the little man, now eager to dissociate himself (and his native town) from such treachery.

– So the wise man goes to the stake for putting his trust in a fool, muses another. There's a lesson in that.

The silence starts on the far side of the square, near the mouth of a side street, then sweeps outward like a wave. Soon everyone is straining to hear. Distantly, a bell tolls; then comes the sound of hoof-beats over cobbles, drawing nearer. In tense silence, the slow cart emerges into the square. The crowd parts before it. Normally this would be the signal for ribald cries and catcalls, but there are none here; instead, every eye is fixed on the towering figure, heavily manacled, standing between two guards – both big, burly men – who scarcely reach his shoulder. A lion's mane of hair falls down his back; his face is stern, noble. As he surveys the crowd, they shrink away, fearing to meet his eye.

The tumbril creaks and groans its way towards the mountainous pyre. The first flakes of snow drift down from the sullen sky. Albanus, oblivious, seems occupied with inward things.

I must think neither of vengeance nor of what is to come: my mind must be clear, unclouded. Where lies my salvation? Close at

9

hand – If I can but catch one's gaze. Who will serve me? The tall one, there.

The young man in the blue bonnet, gazing soulfully at the towering pyre, swivels his head suddenly, like someone called by name – and finds himself looking straight at the condemned man. Their eyes meet.

And lock.

Perhaps the devil will come to fetch him, murmurs someone, giving voice to the thought – the hope? – that has gathered so many here to stand in such tense expectation. The guards hand Albanus down from the cart: hindered by the manacles, he mounts the ladder awkwardly. It is set at an easy angle like a flight of steps against the pile of brushwood. As he makes his slow ascent, the young man in the blue bonnet gazes after him like a dog at its master, awaiting the return of his attention. At last, chain links ringing in the eerie silence, he gains the platform – it is level with the surrounding balconies. The guards bind him to the stake, passing the rope in great loops crisscross about his body and his legs. Only when he is well trussed do they descend, to busy themselves at the pyre's foot. The snow falls thicker now.

Ay, look away, dogs – I am bound and helpless but still you fear my gaze! Yet there is one –

The tall youth in the plumed bonnet stares, wide-eyed.

That yearning look, the pity in his eyes – a fatal sympathy.

The torches are set to the pyre's foot.

I have you now – hold, hold for life!

Grey tongues of smoke curl about the scaffold.

To enter the mind of another: like the first tender moments of love.

The flames rush upwards, crackling.

I fly!

As the figure at the stake slumps forward, the crowd as one breathes out a single, trembling sigh.

Afterwards, the Duke's secretary (whose duty it was to write a faithful account of all that happened) remarked with what calmness the doomed man surveyed the crowd below, like one that looked for an acquaintance there; then, seeming to find the one he sought, bent his gaze upon him, to the exclusion of all else, so that neither the soldiers, putting their torches to the pyre, nor the priest, praying for the salvation of his soul, received any heed from him; and he continued thus intent, even as the flames took hold. Yet all were agreed that long before the fire reached his body – for the pyre was tall, and slow to catch, through the dampness of the season – his spirit had already fled. A noble youth, watching in the crowd, was by pity so overcome that he fell into a swound, and did not recover consciousness until many days had passed.

II – *Forcalquier, France, at the Villa of Ruggiero da Montefeltro, Autumn 1516*

She wakes in the dark with the memory of a scream like a bright light still reverberating in her mind, her heart thudding: a nightmare. How long she sits, bedclothes drawn up to her chin, before the knocking comes, she does not know; but at the sound of the knock she feels a thrill of joy and fear. It is Massimo! He has come to her! Yet how can he dare, with her father and the old man so close at hand? How can he take such a risk? If they find him with her, they will slay him! Driven by fear, she clambers down from her bed, desperate to warn him – and to see him. The flagged floor is cold under her bare feet: she gathers the fur bedcover about her body. The knocking continues, low and urgent.

– Massimo, is that you?

– Open up, quickly!

She draws the bolt and sees that he is fully dressed, a lantern in his hand.

– Massimo, what is it? Why are you here? They will surely kill you!

– Get dressed, gather your things – we must leave at once.

He pushes aside her embraces, hurrying her into the room.

– But my father – the old man –

– Will not hinder us.

A look is exchanged between them: he watches her face closely by the lantern's light, sees wonder there, and a dawning fear.

– Do not be afraid! I am not a murderer. Their own folly has undone them.

Still she hesitates: a look of impatience crosses his face –
what is it now? She gestures, blushing, at her clothes draped
over the chair. He throws up his hands in exasperation.
  – *Beata Vergine!* This is no time for modesty!
But he turns away all the same. She dresses.

Now they are hurrying down the passageway, Massimo
speaking in urgent, hushed tones.
  – I heard them say they planned to use it tonight. I lay
awake a long time but nothing happened. I must have dozed.
Then I thought I heard a scream –
  – I heard it too!
  – And it seemed there was a light, so bright that I was
aware of it through the stone wall, but that must have been
a dream –
  – I dreamt it too, then!
Now they are at the chamber door. She looks at him,
fearful.
  – It's all right. I have already been in. There's nothing
there.
He pushes the door. A pungent brimstone smell fills
their nostrils. As they enter, she could swear she hears a
hollow laugh; but perhaps it is only the wind. The light of
Massimo's lantern shows an empty room, a bare table
standing in the middle. There is a glint of something scattered
on the floor.
  – The philosophical engine! she pronounces the words
carefully, with reverence but without understanding. It's broken!
Something else is glittering there, brilliant in the dark.
  – O, the Stone!
She starts towards it fearfully; Massimo catches her arm.
  – Be careful! Do not touch it! Here, use this!

She makes a nest of the velvet cloth and gathers the stone lovingly, a precious egg. He smiles at her concern: the lantern shows a great chip struck out of the floor where the stone fell. The stone itself is quite unharmed. She holds it up and its many facets catch the light and throw it back.

– How it sparkles! How beautiful it is!

He smiles at that too, a different sort of smile, as at a rival. He bends to gather the scattered pieces of the machine. He examines them carefully: they are intact. It seems the machine has shaken itself apart.

They are in his studio now. She watches (still clutching the stone) as he busies himself gathering the tools of his trade. His movements are swift, certain, decisive. That is what she loves in him: this confidence in everything he does. He stands a moment in front of the unfinished portrait on the easel. Beneath the scarlet turban, the sly face of the old man looks out at him from a blank background with dark, unfathomable eyes.

– Do we have to take *him*? she pleads.

He laughs.

– What, don't you want a memento of your betrothed?

A look of such horror crosses her face that he holds up his hand in apology, then reaches out to stroke her cheek.

– It's all right, he's gone now. You'll never see him again. Or your father.

– Poor papa! But must we take the picture? I'd rather you burnt it!

– It's proof of my skill. If I'm to find a new master, I'll need to show what I can do.

She likes that too: his practicality.

– What about the philosophical engine?

He shakes his head.

- But surely it is very valuable?
- It is too dangerous: I wouldn't trust myself with it. Best leave it here.

She clutches the stone, suddenly fearful.

- But not the Stone? It was promised to me – as my Bride-piece!

He looks at her: so young, so beautiful. One cannot always be wise.

- All right – if I am to keep the bridegroom, you might as well keep his bribe.

He puts the portrait with the rest of his gear, then wraps the pieces of the philosophical engine in oiled cloth and conceals the package in a hidden space in one of the pillars of the great hall.

Dawn is breaking as they make their way down the stony road, a young man, a girl and a laden donkey. At the crossroads he gestures: that is the way to Italy, to home – but there are many artists there already. This is the way to the North: he has heard that artists are in great demand there, especially Italian ones. She smiles and leaves the choice to him, content to follow him to the ends of the earth.

The sun rises.

He draws the donkey to the left.

They go North.

1
Expelled

"A dam' fine pugilist". The headmistress looked at her notes, wondering why she had written that down. It was one of only two entries in the column headed "in favour". The other was "brilliant at languages". Both were from the same source: that crazy old Pruitt woman, who taught the girl classics and, it appeared, every modern language under the sun. The column headed "against" was much more crowded. She sighed, and looked up at the subject of her notes.

Helen De Havilland looked steadily back at her, unflinching.

The headmistress, conscious of being drawn into a battle of wills, returned her attention to the column headed "against":

Aloof, stand-offish, a loner. <u>*NOT A TEAM PLAYER*</u> (this from the games mistress, who thought it the ultimate deficiency of character) *"I sense that Helen is a deeply unhappy child"* (that was the gushing Miss Bunting, for whom a broken nail constituted grounds for counselling) Mmm – unhappiness was not uncommon, in the headmistress's experience, among the children of the very rich (that attending her school might be a factor did not occur to her). What else was there? *Very able academically* (that was less common) *but will not apply herself – entirely without enthusiasm for ANYTHING* !

Really, the exasperation this girl brought out in the staff practically leapt off the page at you. She stole a covert look at Helen, who was now gazing out of the window. Tall and dark-haired, she stood in a classic ballet-dancer's pose, arms behind her back, head tilted, gracefully erect. Such a good-looking girl too, if only she would keep that scowl off her face, mused the headmistress, surprising herself with this irrelevance.

Through the open window, a burst of birdsong came clear into the silence of the room. In the middle distance a gardener trundled a wheelbarrow across the shining lawn.

Helen was wondering at what point she could have decided differently and so avoided being here. At the door of the common room, perhaps? Surely she could have turned back then, as she hesitated, hand on the handle? But no – that hesitation was no more than a drawing of breath, gathering her forces before she stepped onto the stage – she had already made up her mind by then. Earlier maybe, in her room, when she had noticed the drawer in her cabinet not properly shut? She could have ignored that, told herself that she had left it that way, not bothered to look – but even before she looked, she had known what she would find. No, unless you went right back to the beginning and had the housemistress allocate Sophie Petrescu to someone else as a room mate – but even then, Helen was the only one with a space to allocate, now that the wretched Armina had departed, along with the tins of chocolate biscuits that she snuffled her way through, pining for her distant homeland.

So it seemed that, given Sophie Petrescu, it was inevitable that she would end up here. The irony was that she actually liked the girl, found in her for the first time a kindred spirit, one that shared her mordant wit and appreciated her cruelly accurate impersonations of her class-mates and teachers. Live-wire Sophie, with her extraordinary combination of skin like soft brown sugar, weird red-brown hair, one eye green the other blue – Sophie the human firework.

Sophie the traitor.

Sophie the thief.

In the common room, Helen understood the scene before her instantly, as in a dream. They might have been posing for a painting: the Ambassador's Daughter on the big green sofa, draped with her fawning acolytes; at her right hand, in the place of honour, nestled under her proprietorial arm, Sophie, smiling.

The Ambassador's Daughter allowed herself a slight smile too as Helen entered: she had waited a long time for this moment. Her free hand lay in her lap, and as Helen stepped into the room she raised it in front of her, holding – as a priest might hold an icon – a distinctive oblong of ultramarine silk.

Helen's diary.

The price that Sophie had paid for entry into the charmed circle.

The Ambassador's Daughter rose slowly to her feet, relishing the moment, relishing her power – every eye in the room was on her, waiting to see what she would do next. She held the diary up like the Statue of Liberty's torch. Yes, she thought, I have waited a long time for this, and I shall have my due – I shall have tears.

Helen advanced towards her rapidly, with a curious bounding gait, and only when she was almost within touching distance did it occur to the Ambassador's Daughter, with a sudden chill feeling, that she might have made a serious mistake: there was not in Helen's face the least hint of fear, or the pleading look she had expected – there was only a furious implacable will that radiated from her like a magnetic force. Seeing Helen move her right hand as if to snatch the diary, she leaned back, holding it out of her reach, pointing her chin defiantly – and so presented the perfect target for the swift left-handed blow which cracked into her jaw and dropped her like a poleaxed ox.

The robust Mlle Souterelle, an advocate of physical aggression on the playing field, squealed in dismay to see it in the common room; but the decrepit-looking Miss Pruitt, who had a soft spot for Helen and had never cared for the Ambassador's Daughter, gave a spontaneous Bravo! (which she later excused as a sneeze) and observed (with the air of one who had seen a few in her time) that it was a very fine left hook indeed.

And now the headmistress, with Helen in front of her, weighed the matter in the balance: on the one scale, the Ambassador's Daughter – it was fortunate the jaw was not broken, or there might have been a legal issue – with her capacity to summon outraged battalions of ambassadorial connections; on the other – well, the De Havilland girl was certainly rich, undoubtedly well-connected – an old family, too, but for that very reason unlikely to demur at her decision: it was the girl they would blame, not the school. The parents were not on the scene either – mother in America; father – wasn't he something of a ne'er-do-well? It was aunts she had to deal with, and experience told her that as a rule aunts were less trouble than parents in matters of this sort. She pursed her lips and looked Helen in the eye.

– Well, have you anything to say for yourself?

A long silence: Helen, it appeared, had nothing to say for herself. She stared steadily back at the headmistress, unabashed, entirely self-sufficient. The headmistress felt a sudden access of irritation at this cool defiance.

– I have not time to waste on matters as straightforward as this. You are to be expelled forthwith. I will communicate my decision to your guardians directly. I suggest you go and pack.

Just for a moment, before Helen turned away, the headmistress thought she saw, not in her mouth – which remained set in a sullen line – but in her eye, the faintest twinkle of what might have been a smile.

*

Helen, returning to her room, was surprised to find an ill-wrapped package on her bed. A rough scrap of paper had been taped to it, bearing a single word in Sophie's unmistakable left-handed scrawl: SORRY.

Helen lifted the package with two fingers, as though it were something distasteful, and dropped it in the wastepaper bin: then just to make certain, she moved the bin to the centre of the floor where Sophie would see it as soon as she entered the room. Then she busied herself with packing, all the time keeping an ear open for returning footsteps.

When she was done and Sophie had not appeared, Helen reviewed the situation dispassionately. She had a long train journey ahead of her, and there was just a chance that the package might contain something to eat, such as chocolates. If not, she could always throw it out the window. After a brief consideration, she retrieved it and stuffed it in the outside pocket of her bag. Sophie might be a traitor and a thief, but chocolate is chocolate.

2
Art Appreciation

Only when the streetlights came on with that pinky warm-up glow that precedes the yellow sodium glare did Jake realise how late it was. In a panic, he began to run, and that was his salvation: as he rounded the corner of the street, he saw that his mother had abandoned the house and was patrolling the pavement, trying (unsuccessfully) to disguise her anxious watching as a casual taking of the evening air. When he arrived in front of her, breathless and in a lather of sweat, his penitence was already evident; he had only to hang his head in face of the tidal wave of rebuke that engulfed him.

Where had he been all this time? What did he mean by coming home at this hour? What had he been up to? Didn't he know how worried they had been? Did he realise his tea was ruined? These questions were fired at him with such rapidity that there was barely time for him to insert an abject mutter of "Sorry, Mum" before the next one came at him.

His mother had clearly been storing up her ammunition for a while, and it was a long time before she had expended all the possible ways of bringing home to her erring son the depths of his iniquity.

That had its advantages, because by the time she was done Jake had his excuse prepared.

– I'm sorry Mum, I had to go see Mr. Macintosh, and afterwards I was talking to this girl, and I really didn't notice what time it was.

– This girl? What girl?

Jake saw at once that it was a mistake not to have provided a name, but supplying one also had its perils – his mother's network of acquaintances was enormous, her ability to supply the family tree of any one of his classmates to the third generation quite unnerving.

– Sara – I don't know her second name. She's new, he added, to be on the safe side.

Jake did not like lying, especially to his mother, though he did find it necessary from time to time, so he always tried to build his fabrications on some foundation of truth, and as his mother, radiating displeasure, shepherded him up the garden path (as though he might make a sudden bid for escape before he reached the house) he reflected that at least five-sixths of his explanation was true: he had indeed been summoned to see Mr. Macintosh, his English teacher, and after that he *had* been talking to a girl (well, sort of) and he genuinely had not noticed the time; and her name *was* Sara, and she *was* new, in a way.

The only lie was about her second name. He knew that well enough.

Wilbright.

To be precise, Miss Wilbright.

She was his art teacher.

Miss Wilbright was new, as Jake had said: she had arrived that Autumn in a storm of sensation that had never quite abated. Her predecessor, mild, middle-aged Mr. Finch (a married man with grown-up children) had for some reason driven his car into the Clyde on the eve of the October holiday, having been seen shortly before in the company of a mysterious redhead half his age. The official verdict was death by misadventure; the popular one was somewhat juicier.

At school, the popular verdict on Miss Wilbright was "seriously weird, even for an art teacher." Her impact could be judged from the deputy head's remark to a colleague: "if any girl came to school looking like that, she'd be sent home." In dress, she favoured multiple layers of what must have started life as underclothes or night attire, now dyed in unlikely combinations of purple, black, crimson, acid green and peacock blue; the longest of these stopped well short of her knees, exposing between their lacy hems and the tops of her scarlet eighteen-hole Doc Marten boots a substantial length of athletic, well-muscled leg clad in tights that were cobweb-patterned, coarse fishnet, hooped in bright colours or severe black-and-white, or (on special occasions) spangled.

Her long tangle of blue-black hair made a striking contrast with her chalky face and eyes of impossible brilliant green; purple lipstick and nail varnish, sundry piercings (including a jewelled nose-stud) and a shoulder tattoo (of a compass-like symbol) rounded off her appearance. The fact that she was rumoured to be a practising pagan (in a Catholic school) added to her fascination. She had an unusually deep, husky voice that made a simple "good morning" sound like

24

an indecent proposal. One half of the school thought her ultimately cool, the other mad, although there was a middle ground that held both views.

Jake was in that middle ground: Miss Wilbright fascinated him, but frightened him a little too, especially when she began to show a marked personal interest in him. It had begun in a casual enough way – she would ask his opinion of a painting or a piece of sculpture, and always treated his response with serious interest, which was flattering. Then she praised his drawing and painting, and would often take considerable trouble to show him how he could improve this or that aspect of it. There was no doubt that, beneath the bizarre exterior, she was an excellent teacher – she knew her subject thoroughly, and could engender an enthusiasm for it in the most unlikely souls: someone who dressed as she did could easily have been dismissed as a clown, but she had a formidable personality, and in her class there were no discipline problems, even from the most notorious hard cases.

It was in the New Year that she had started the Art Appreciation classes after school, for the hand-picked few, mostly drawn from her sixth-year art class; Jake was the only one from lower down the school, and he was considerably surprised and pleased to be asked along, not least because the girls in sixth-year art were reckoned among the prime talent in the school, and to be able to claim acquaintance with them and have them smile and greet him in the corridor made him the envy of his class-mates.

Gradually Jake became aware that he spent more time in Art Appreciation than anyone else – he tended to be there first, and he was always last out, because Miss Wilbright invariably enlisted his help in tidying up; and often, just as he was about to go, she would ask him "to just take a look at this" or "what do you think of that?" and produce something for his consideration: a picture of some famous work of art, or a piece she was working on herself; these impromptu sessions could delay him half an hour or more.

Usually, that was not a problem, because his parents were quite happy provided they knew where he was (or was supposed to be) and were delighted that Jake was involved in such a range of extra-curricular activities: Football practice on Monday, Badminton on Tuesday, Drama on Wednesday, Thursday for Art Appreciation.

But today was Friday, and this Art Appreciation class had been unscheduled, one-to-one.

Jake had gone, after the final bell, to Mr. Macintosh's room, where they had had a slightly weird conversation. Mr. Macintosh (also new that session – he had come in mid-November) had all Jake's English work spread out on the desk; he said he was particularly interested in a character Jake used as the hero in his stories, a man called Stephen Bishop, a millionaire art collector – there was something familiar about him, said Mr. Macintosh. Jake, thinking he was being accused of plagiarism, defended himself staunchly – Bishop was modelled on a real person, his friend Stephen Langton ("Bishop" was a joke on the fact that there had once been an Archbishop of Canterbury with that name) who did happen to be a millionaire art collector. Maybe that was it, said Macintosh – might he have met this Mr. Langton sometime? Did he live in Glasgow? No, said Jake, he lived near Cambridge, close to the village of Manorhampton, where he had this fabulous place, Silk House –

And it was just at that point that they had both become aware of Miss Wilbright, hovering in the doorway. The sun was directly behind her, so that her face was dark but ringed with a nimbus of sunlit hair; it shone through her filmy garments so that Jake could clearly see the curvaceous outline of her body underneath.

– I just wanted a word with Jake, if you've finished with him.

I'm popular today, thought Jake.

– O, yes – on you go, Giacometti. Thanks for clearing that point up for me.

Jake followed Miss Wilbright out the door, still puzzled by his interview with Macintosh. Had he really come to the point, or did Miss Wilbright interrupt him? She had paused to let him catch up. He approached her with that familiar tingling feeling, somewhere below the region of his stomach. She was wearing perfume with a smoky sort of incense-like smell. She fixed him with her impossible emerald eyes and gave a smile of complicity.

– I thought you might want rescuing.

She nodded in the direction of Macintosh's room.

–O, yes – thanks. He was just asking me something about one of my stories.

– Does he – take a special interest in your work?

Alarm bells started to go off in Jake's head: a teacher being subtle about something. Was she trying to warn him off Macintosh?

– Not really, Miss – if fact not at all before now.

– You can call me Sara: we're out of school hours now.

If this was supposed to put Jake at his ease and win his confidence, it had the opposite effect. He felt suddenly awkward, acutely aware of how close she was to him.

– You don't have to if you don't want to, she said with a smile. I just find all this "miss" and "sir" business so stuffy and old-fashioned.

– I suppose it is, really.

He relaxed again.

– There was something I wanted to show you. I'm really excited about it.

They were in the art room now, one of Jake's favourite places in the school: everything here was so messy and undisciplined. There were all sorts of fascinating things lying about, stuff that was used for drawing classes: bits of old machinery; a fishing net and some bright yellow floats; a stuffed fox; there was even a small crocodile hanging from the ceiling, which gave the room the air of an apothecary's shop. On the wall were a mixture of paintings that people in the school had done – some of them really good – and big posters for various art exhibitions.

Miss Wilbright was fiddling with the blinds.

– Close the door, would you Jake? We need darkness for this.

Jake closed the door and stood, hesitant, by the light switch. Now Miss Wilbright (Sara!) was working at something she had put on a clear space on the desk. Her dark hair fell forward over her pale face; her arms were like ivory under her lacy shawl.

– Kill the light, would you?

Jake switched off the light. He felt an odd tightening in his throat. What were they going to do?

– Now, come over here.

Jake was about to protest that he could not see, when a soft glow appeared in the middle of the room. An *effulgence*, thought Jake, that's what that is. It seemed to be coming from whatever was on the desk, a fuzzy golden hemisphere; Miss Wilbright stood behind it, and it lit her from below, making an eerie pattern of golden patches and dark pockets of shadow. Jake edged cautiously towards her, aware of the jutting angles of desks in his path.

– Sit down.

Jake took a seat, and Miss Wilbright sat also, on a stool, he guessed, because she was higher up than he was. She leaned towards him; her face was like a golden mask suspended in mid air. Her hands rested on something rectangular and upright, covered in a cloth. In front of it was the source of light, a cloud of luminous mist trapped under an inverted glass bowl. It was bright enough to hold the eye, but not dazzling.

– Now, here's what I want you to look at.

She drew back the cloth.

– You need the subdued light to see it properly.

– It's beautiful.

It was a picture of a child, a girl of about seven or so, painted with extraordinary vivacity and spontaneity: she turned towards the viewer just as she might towards a camera for a snapshot; she wore a formal dress of blue silk – a miniature version of something an adult might wear – and round her neck was a rope of heavy, lustrous pearls, with below that a huge ruby pendant on a silver chain. Her eyes looked directly out at you, with a sort of humorous challenge; her mouth seemed just about to laugh. She stood on a balcony, with a marble balustrade behind her, and beyond that, a fantastic landscape of pointed green hills under a blue-green sky; to one side, a small table stood, half concealed behind a heavy damask curtain of rich orange-brown, caught into a swag with a rope of red-gold silk. The combination of minute detail with the soft, diffuse light was wonderfully vivid, making it seem not a painting at all, but more like the view from a window: it was like sitting in the dark interior of the same house, looking out at the girl in the sunlight. Then he saw that on the table a hand rested, clad in a gauntlet of dark green silk, the fingers adorned with heavy jewelled rings. The presence of the hand lent the picture an air of mystery: it had a suggestion of masculine force about it, hinting that someone of great power was sitting behind the curtain. Jake felt drawn towards the balcony, as if the girl was beckoning him ...

He was aware of a soft voice talking, but could not pay heed to the words: the picture held him rapt, utterly absorbed.

*

And it was true, what he had told his mother – he really had not noticed the time passing. It was only now, lying on his bed, that he realised there were two whole hours of his life he could not account for. Where had he been?

Where, indeed?

3
The Stone of Sorrow

The, bus, with a farewell glint of its rear window, slipped over the distant brow of the dead straight road, taking the twenty-first century with it. A bird in the woods sent up a sudden chakkering cry that ceased as abruptly as it started, leaving the silence deeper than before. Gerald De Havilland surveyed the dark ranks of forest brooding on either side of the road beneath a sunlit sky piled high with masses of white cloud.

Lithuania, now, he thought. Or then.

Out here, in a countryside reduced to its essential, ancient elements – this road, these trees, that sky – the distinction between past and present blurred. He could easily believe that somewhere in that wood might be an Aurochs, one of the giant wild oxen that had survived here (protected by royal decree) a thousand years after they became extinct in the rest of Europe. Once, this tiny obscure Baltic republic had partnered Poland in the Commonwealth of Two Nations, a vast dominion that for centuries was the most powerful in the Western world; had been the last bastion of paganism, too, in ancient Samogitia, well into the fifteenth century.

These trees would have been here then, and that sky, and probably this road too. Screwing up his eyes against the glare, he visualized the little entourage: a cart, perhaps, drawn by a mule; or more likely just a mule, the man leading it, the girl on its back; or perhaps both walking, the mule laden with their luggage...and in that luggage...he smiled at himself, trying to conjure the past to make his present desires come true. Yet it was surely this same road they travelled, Massimo Mancino, the young Italian artist, and the girl he had eloped with – barely fourteen, she must have been, younger than Helen – a thousand miles and more they journeyed together from the Villa Ruggiero in the South of France; but what did they bring with them?

He knew well enough what they had left behind – the Alchemist's Machine, dismantled and wrapped in oiled cloth and hidden in a hollow pillar of the villa's great hall; and something they had taken with them too – the unfinished portrait of Ruggiero da Montefeltro that Mancino had later completed as The Secret of the Alchemist, containing the clue to the whereabouts of the Machine – but what else? That was the question.

When the answer to it had first suggested itself to him and Stephen Langton – in the front room at Silk House – it had seemed a great deal more convincing than it did now.

– Plans, said Stephen. They must have had plans.

– It's hard to see how they could have built it otherwise, agreed De Havilland.

The Alchemist's Machine, assembled now after many painstaking months, sat on the table between them, evidently complete yet completely non-functioning. It resembled nothing so much as the skeleton of some curious creature, though what precisely was difficult to say: there was something bird-like about it. Only an egg-shaped void at the heart of it offered any hope.

– That space, now, said Stephen. Something must go there, surely?

– Those prongs look as though they were meant to hold something.

– But what?

– A battery, maybe? said De Havilland, joking.

– Could be – could well be! Something that is consumed or spent when the machine is operated – that would explain why it wasn't with the rest!

– But how do we find out?

Which brought them back to the plans. Reflecting on it, De Havilland saw that what had seemed hard logic at the time now looked more like wishful thinking: if there was something missing, then the plans would show it; so there *must* be plans, and Mancino *must* have taken them with him, since he hadn't left them behind. Of course. And by the same token, they *must* have survived nearly five centuries of strife, with continual changes of borders and rulers, frequent wars and all the mayhem and destruction that went with them, in order to be discovered at the first attempt by yours truly, Gerald De Havilland, posing as a Professor of Fine Art from one of the lesser-known Cambridge Colleges. Yes indeed.

His gloomy meditations were interrupted by a distant sound. Turning towards it, he saw a vehicle of unusual shape approaching: only when it was quite close was he able to resolve its puzzling appearance into its constituent parts: below a divided windscreen, two huge separate headlamps like twin moons flanked a vertically-slatted upright radiator, with flaring wing-like mudguards sprouting on either side. The distinctive shape of the top of the grille – a curve with two flat shoulders – proclaimed it to be a Packard, from just before the Second World War, he guessed.

It glided to a halt beside him, muttering quietly. It was a very dark shade of blue. The paint was dull with age; there was a coat of arms on the rear door. The driver emerged, a small, dapper man in an old-fashioned chauffeur's uniform, lavender grey in colour, with peaked cap, polished knee-boots and a double row of buttons on the jacket. For all the brave polish on his boots he had a slightly threadbare, down-at-heel appearance, as one who had known better days and strove to keep the memory alive.

– Professeur De Havilland? he asked in a distinctly French accent.

– The same, said De Havilland.

He held up his raincoat-draped briefcase like a badge of office in what he hoped was an appropriately professorial gesture. The chauffeur held open the door to the rear compartment (it hinged backwards) and De Havilland stepped up onto the running board and into the cavernous interior. The passenger compartment had the same run-down air as the chauffeur: it had once been luxurious, but now the leather was cracked, the veneers peeling; there was a musty smell that suggested the car had only recently been rescued from long neglect. Still, it was comfortable enough, and, with the heavy division between him and the driver, remarkably quiet.

He had begun to doze, daydreaming visions of finding the plans folded in some great ledger, when the Packard swung off the road and plunged into the trees, onto what seemed no more than a woodland track: it was entirely grass-covered, but unusually smooth – it might have been a stone pavement that was now overgrown, or maybe the Packard had very good suspension. They had covered a mile or so in thickening twilight when they stopped; the chauffeur got out and with the aid of a flashlight unchained and opened a huge pair of ramshackle gates. The top of them was lost in the darkness above; from the pillars on either side, carved heraldic animals glowered down at them. The chauffeur drove through and then secured the gates behind them. It seemed an unnecessary precaution.

The light was failing rapidly now, and the great beams of the headlights swept the way ahead, illuminating the tree-trunks on either side like rows of pillars. Then they picked out an ivy-covered wall, which he took at first for the façade of the house – he glimpsed windows among the shaggy growth – until the car drove through it, under a broad archway, and into a vast courtyard. He glimpsed a massive ornamental fountain in the centre as they rumbled over flagstones, then the headlights raked the lower story of a looming mass of building at the far end, showing tall shuttered windows on either side of a grand portico with a huge studded door that dwarfed the figure standing in front of it, holding up a light that shone with a soft yellow glow.

The chauffeur sprang nimbly out to open his door while the light-bearing figure came down the steps towards them, revealing itself to be a small elderly woman, of the same vintage as the chauffeur, perhaps his wife – there was something in their exchange of greetings that suggested a long-established domesticity. They spoke in French. The lamp the woman carried was an old-fashioned storm-lantern, and the way she held it up, peering ahead of her into the dark, suggested a figure from an allegorical painting. She led them up the steps to the studded door, the chauffeur bringing up the rear with De Havilland's travelling bag.

Entering the hall, he was arrested by an extraordinary apparition: suspended in the gloom, some distance away, three children were watching him – they appeared to be hovering in mid air. That, and their flaxen hair, put him in mind of angels. It was difficult to determine their sex: all wore their hair long, and it was too dark to see their clothes. The tallest of the three had a more masculine edge to his features. For a moment he stood, paused in mid-stride, expecting one of them to speak.

Then gradually his eyes grew accustomed to the dark, and he saw that the hall was the full height of the house with a grand stair at the far end – on the landing of this stair a painting of three children, many times larger than life size, was lit by moonlight from a window high up. Near at hand, the feeble lantern shed a ring of light, beyond which he could guess at tall carved furnishings and the heavy gilt frames of large paintings; here and there the light glinted on the eyes and teeth of stuffed animals. Halfway along the panelled wall the woman opened a concealed door and ushered him into a room entirely lit by candles.

His Serene Highness Prince Steponas Algirdas Vytautas-Geminidas was an unusually tall man, nearer seven foot than six, with an angular thinness that recalled a large wading bird. He had a fine head of white hair, and might have been any age from sixty to over eighty.

– Professor De Havilland, how pleasant to meet you! Welcome to my ancient home.

His voice was pleasant and musical, with only a trace of

foreign accent. He gestured about him with a long hand.

– You must forgive the candles, they are rather more than an old-world affectation. Our electrical generator has developed a fault which has so far proved beyond the ingenuity of Maurice to repair. Still, it is a kindly light. Won't you please sit down?

Looking around, De Havilland could see that it was a room that needed kind lighting: the walls were cracked and peeling, and in more than one place the plaster had come away altogether, showing strips of lath. The Prince was clearly following his train of thought.

– There is much that needs to be done, I fear, to make the old place fit to receive visitors again. We have managed to secure you a watertight bedroom, you will be glad to hear, and Sylvie has set a fire to drive out the damp. She has been preparing ferociously all day: you are the first visitor this house has seen in many years.

– I am honoured.

– You are too kind. May I offer you a glass of Tokay?

– Thank you.

– Yes, it is a long business, seeking reparation – only the lawyers get fat from it. First the Soviets – then the Nazis – then again the Soviets; now the democrats. There are many things we will never get back: we are fortunate to have recovered this estate intact. But we are patient; even in the darkest hour there is hope. Seventy years might seem a long time, but our family has lived here for seven hundred. We have known hard times before, but our time will come around again – it always does. The Thousand-year Reich lasted barely twelve; communism crumbled in a lifetime; democracy is daily exposed as a corrupt sham, the tool of big business and the global corporations. How long before that, too, withers? Then people will turn to what they trusted in the past, the old families.

For a moment, the illusion was complete: the tall figure in the firelight, hand on the back of a chair, strong aristocratic face looking proudly to the future, awaiting the people's call. But only for a moment: then reality crowded in – the peeling plaster, the guttering candles, the ancient musty Packard, the huge decaying house with its two threadbare servants. This man is seriously mad, thought De Havilland.

– But you must forgive me: politics is hardly what has brought you here. "The Influence of Italy on the Art of the Baltic States" – that is correct, is it not?

– Indeed yes, said De Havilland. (As a token of his serious intent, he took out his remaining academic prop – a pair of gold-rimmed half-moon glasses – and put them on.) Of course the whole world knows of Bacciarelli and his workshop, he said, in lecturing tones, but that was in the eighteenth century, and I am minded to go further back, to the reign of Bona Sforza.

– Stirring times, said the Prince.

– Bartolomeo Berecci, of course, is of primary interest, as is Francesco Fiorentino; Santi Gucci too –

He watched the Prince carefully as he said these names, and judged that he recognized them, but found them of no special interest. He took his glasses off again, polishing them, and mused,

– But it is so often the lesser figures who turn out to be more interesting– if only we knew more about them! That colourful character Flavio Portinari, for instance – I'm almost certain he came here on his wide wanderings; then there's the likes of Ambrosio del Foscolo, a rather shadowy figure, or Massimo Mancino, of whom the sum total of our knowledge amounts to the surmise – based on his name – that he was left-handed...

– Massimo Mancino? I think we may be able to tell you a little more than that about him –

– O really? said De Havilland, with no evident interest. Bramante too – if we could establish that *he* came here now, that would be something!

He was aware, with some satisfaction, of mounting agitation on the Prince's part.

– Do you have anything on Bramante, do you think? he queried innocently.

– On Bramante, no – I do not really think so. But Mancino now –

– So little is known about him: it's by no means certain he was even here.

– O, he was here all right, of that I can assure you!

– Indeed? De Havilland allowed himself a flicker of interest. To establish *that* for certain would be a definite contribution – small, but definite!

– I can say with some authority that he was here. My ancestor, the Archduke Vilkas, employed him.

– Is that so? But I expect that there is very little in the way of documentary evidence –

– On the contrary, there is a substantial archive. You see, there are other reasons why Mancino is remembered in our family – besides his skill as an artist, I mean.

De Havilland raised his eyebrows expectantly, but now it was the Prince who seemed inclined to create a little suspense.

– But I am forgetting my manners – you have had a long

journey, and will want to freshen up before dinner! I took the liberty of instructing Sylvie to draw you a bath as soon as you appeared: our plumbing is rather antiquated, I fear, but I expect it will be ready by now.

He tugged an ornamental silk bell-pull by the fireplace, and in a short while the faithful Maurice appeared in answer to the summons.

The bathroom was a gothic experience, the bath looming through a candlelit fog of steam like the hull of some great ship. De Havilland emerged considerably relaxed and refreshed three-quarters of an hour later and managed to find the dining room at only the third attempt. He was surprised to find that his host was not alone – seated at the table was a woman of uncertain age who bore a striking family resemblance to the Prince. She might have been called beautiful, in a glacial sort of way, though there was a curious lack of animation about her face.

– My daughter, Alexandra.

She bowed, and gave a strange, vacant smile. Throughout the meal – which was delicious – the Prince included her in the conversation, addressing remarks to her, but she made no response and spent most of her time staring into space. She ate and drank what was set in front of her in a mechanical way, without apparent relish, and showed no interest at all in the stranger at their table.

His host seemed to find nothing remarkable in this behaviour. He was an excellent conversationalist, and his talk ranged from his political ambitions – which were somewhat idealistic – to Lithuanian history and his family's role in it, a subject he managed to make remarkably interesting. Only when his daughter had left them – she rose abruptly and departed without a word when Maurice brought the brandy and cigars – did he return to the subject of Mancino.

– You will have seen the portrait in the hall – the three children?

– Yes indeed, very striking! Is that by Mancino?

– No, but it is a good starting point to explain his involvement with my family. Did you have a chance to look at it closely?

De Havilland drew on his cigar and sent a cloud of blue smoke curling up towards the ceiling. His mind raced: was this some sort of test of his credentials? Perhaps there was something special about the painting that he should have remarked. He had in fact stopped to look at it on his way to the dining room.

– The light was not very good, I'm afraid, but I could make out that they were singularly handsome children – a brother and two sisters, I suppose?

A little flattery never goes amiss, he thought. Besides, it was true – they were very striking. The Prince smiled.

– Indeed. They are beautiful, are they not? Angelic would not be an exaggeration.

He blew out a long stream of smoke and gave De Havilland an odd, sidelong look.

– They are the children of my direct ancestor, Algirdas. The boy, Stanislaus, almost certainly murdered his father, and colluded with his sister – Marisa, the younger one – in the murder of their Uncle, the Archduke Vilkas. Marisa later went mad, and was confined to a tower for the last twenty years of her life, which ended when she fell from the parapet – though it is more than likely that her brother threw her off. Throughout his life he was afflicted by murderous rages and it is probable

41

that his own children poisoned him, with the aid of his wife. The other sister, Anna, was simpleminded – she remained like a child all her life – but she was at least harmless. Their mother, Amelia, killed herself.

– Good God! What an appalling catalogue! What happened?

The Prince gave him a shrewd look, drawing on his cigar until the ash glowed red.

– A curse.

De Havilland returned his look, but forced himself to say nothing. After a time, the Prince went on.

– The family had unwittingly acquired an object which drove its possessors to insanity and murder.

He cocked an eye at De Havilland to see how seriously he took this.

– That at least was the popular account, one that my ancestors actively fostered – in fact, they almost certainly invented it. It is always so much easier to blame external forces – what is it Shakespeare says? "To lay our goatish disposition to the charge of a star".

De Havilland, cigar in hand, puckered his brow in what he hoped was a donnish frown.

– Do I infer that here "the fault, dear Brutus, is not in our stars, but in ourselves"?

The Prince beamed at him. I'm doing well, thought De Havilland. Thank God for a flypaper memory, and a good prison library.

– My ancestor Archduke Vilkas – the name means "Wolf" – was a man of prodigious energy: a real renaissance man. He built this house, and transformed the estates from mediaeval feudalism to something extraordinarily advanced

42

for his day – this was in the sixteenth century, in Bona Sforza's time. He was avid for all the new ideas that were beginning to reach this part of the world from Southern Europe, especially Italy, and his court, like King Zygmund's in Warsaw, was full of foreigners – artists, engineers, scientists, philosophers.

His one sadness was that he had no children, so he had adopted his younger brother's son, Algirdas, as his heir. Now this Algirdas was a wild youth, a terrible heartbreaker, forever dallying with young maidens, then discarding them when he grew bored. One of his victims was an Italian girl, Elena, the daughter of an artist at Vilkas's court. She was very young – only twelve or thirteen – and her mind must have been affected: soon after he abandoned her, she ran off, and was never seen again. Her mother, who was pregnant at the time, was demented with grief. She scoured the countryside, searching for her daughter, then she too disappeared. Everyone was sure she had done away with herself, but over a year later she turned up again, having given birth to twins, a boy and a girl.

Now, as the years went by, Vilkas's lavish spending began to take its toll – the estate was nearly bankrupt. He was desperate for his nephew to make a suitable marriage, not only to secure the succession, but also to bring a much-needed injection of capital. Unfortunately, there were not many suitable candidates. Then he was approached by the mother of Elena, the girl his nephew had ruined, with an extraordinary proposition: if Algirdas would marry her second daughter, Amelia – the twin – she would bestow on her a priceless dowry.

Vilkas was inclined at first to be scornful – the woman was mad, had never got over the death of her first daughter, and what she proposed seemed further proof of that; besides, where would she, an artist's wife, come by a priceless dowry? But then she took Vilkas aside and showed him something, and he saw in it the salvation of his fortunes. So Algirdas and Amelia wed, and her dowry passed into our family.

The Prince drew on his cigar and sent another cloud of blue smoke to the ceiling. De Havilland leaned forward in his chair.

– The dowry, I take it, was the bringer of the curse?

– Quite. And truly, in a way. Picture the scene: the family is gathered for the banquet to celebrate the christening of the third child, Marisa. There are the usual toasts and speeches. Then Amelia's mother, the Italian woman, stands up. Everyone is startled, because for years she has scarcely uttered a word. She begins in a conventional enough way, saying that for much of her life she has longed for only one thing and now that she has it she can die happy. Of course everyone thinks she is referring to her daughter's marriage, now blessed with a new child.

Another dramatic pause: more fragrant smoke drawn in, then exhaled with exquisite slowness.

– Then she tells them what the one thing is: vengeance.

– Vengeance?

– Vengeance for her daughter Elena, vengeance on the man who ruined her – Algirdas, of course, as everyone there knew. The hall is in consternation and uproar: what does she mean to do – harm the children in some way? Her next utterance takes them by surprise, it is so unexpected: I only ever had two children, she tells them: my son, who is dead now, and my beloved Elena. She points at Algirdas. Elena who died in the wilderness giving birth to that man's child.

He paused, to watch the incredulous realization steal

over De Havilland's face.

— No, he breathed, mouthing the word rather than speaking it.

— Yes, said the Prince. The child survived, and she raised it as her own – raised it to be the instrument of her revenge.

— My God! She tricked him into marrying his own daughter? It's pure Greek tragedy!

— The effects were devastating. Poor Amelia, learning how she had been used by the woman she thought was her mother, committed suicide. Algirdas never recovered: he felt he was accursed. Along with everyone else, he was convinced that the offspring of their union must be monsters, with the result that he turned two of them into monsters by the way he treated them. Ironically, it was probably only the middle child – Anna, the simple one – who had the sort of genetic defect that can result in such cases.

He caught the look on De Havilland's face.

— Yes, it is an hereditary defect – the condition is a very rare one: it is named after our family. It surfaces every generation or so. It is what afflicts my own daughter, Alexandra.

— I am sorry.

The Prince made an eloquent gesture of hopeless acceptance.

— It is just, as they say, one of these things. But no doubt you are wondering what all this has to do with Massimo Mancino?

— He was the father of Elena, the girl Algirdas ruined – the husband of the Italian woman?

— You have it!

The Italian woman: her own name was lost to history.

De Havilland had a sudden vision of her, setting out resolutely from the Villa Ruggiero to follow in the footsteps of her lover, a slender girl younger than his own daughter: if she could have seen where that would lead her, would she have gone on?

– And the accursed dowry?

The Prince rose and went to the sideboard, returning with a square object draped with dark cloth. He removed the cloth to reveal an unremarkable metal box, faded red in colour, the paint flaking to show bare metal underneath. He put it on the table in front of De Havilland.

– It is fortunate for my story you arrived when you did – another week and this would be gone, on its way to Paris. I have arranged for an auction house there to sell it for me next month. If I am to restore the fortunes of my house, I fear I must liquidate some of my assets. Please, do open it. It is not locked.

De Havilland flicked the catches and lifted the lid. Reposed on a bed of rumpled black velvet was a magnificent crystal, the size and shape of a small egg, its surface cut in myriad facets that caught and threw back the light of the candles and the fire in iridescent sparks. It was clasped between two hands, exquisitely wrought in gold, which seemed to offer it to the onlooker. The Prince smiled at his amazement.

– Behold, he said, The Stone of Sorrow.

4
The Warlock's Tower

The little green car dropped into first gear to round the hairpin then laboured harshly up the return slope, climbing higher and higher into the Carpathian Mountains. The driver, a small man with a scrubby brown beard, perched on the edge of his seat, the steering wheel pulled almost to his chest, head straining forward as if it were thick fog he drove through and not this bright, pleasant morning tinged with frost. On the seat beside him was a large old-fashioned doctor's bag. Presently the road reached an ancient narrow bridge, hump-backed and ill-suited to motor traffic; the little car groaned its way over at walking pace then toiled up the short slope to the village.

The villagers would be there already, just over the rise, crowded into the cobbled space before the inn, drawn by the sound of the approaching car. He could picture them pressing forward, eager to flag the stranger down, to warn him that the road beyond was impassable – blocked by fallen trees or rocks, or else a broken bridge, or it had subsided – maybe all of these at once, such was their anxiety to prevent further progress, to draw the stranger in to enjoy their simple hospitality, then presently send him back down the valley laden with their blessings (including plastic bottles of the fierce local spirit), puzzled but delighted by the warmth of their welcome and their concern for his well-being.

As the green car breasted the rise, he saw them move into the road, then check themselves as they recognized first the car, then its driver; he saw them draw back as one, the look on their faces changing from eager anxiety to fear. Several blessed themselves; others held their hands downwards with the middle two fingers curled into the palm, the outer two pointing to the ground, the ancient sign to ward off the evil eye. The little man sneered as he rattled past them without slackening his already modest speed. Superstitious fools!

But as the car climbed out of the deep cleft of the valley into the stony heights above he felt his own fear grow like a cancer in his stomach, and spread through his whole body. A huge feeling of oppression weighed on him, crushing him down, almost a physical force – indeed, the little car appeared to feel it too, gasping to a halt just below the brow of the final hill, where it rested for a time, seeming to gather all its small strength for the final push. The man sat, rigid and sweating, for some minutes before he felt able to continue.

The car emerged onto a flat stony plateau ringed by craggy hills. The road – now little more than a track – ran straight ahead to its end, a distinctive spur of rock reared up from the hill-slope and surmounted by a squat turret. Such maps as marked it called it the Warlock's Tower, though its local names were more graphic and obscene. The little man, jaws clenched, hunched behind the wheel, forced the car on the last couple of miles. When he killed the engine he was assailed on all sides by an immense sense of desolation: not a bird called; not so much as a blade of grass seemed alive in this stony wilderness. He took his bag and eased himself reluctantly out of the car, closing the door with exaggerated care, afraid to break the windy silence.

The spur of rock had long ago been burrowed into, hollowed out to make a dwelling place of sorts: a heavy wooden door was set into the foot of it. Before this the little doctor stood, bag held defensively at his chest, making a conscious effort to stand upright. Presently, the door swung open; the doctor stepped through, and it closed behind him, without human agency. The hall within was vaulted, the walls of bare stone, unadorned, the floor stone flags. The temperature was several degrees lower than outside. The man shivered, but not from the cold. Though a frequent visitor here of late, he could not free himself from the feeling he had on entering of being stripped naked under the gaze of a pitiless scrutiny. He took refuge in his own insignificance: he knew himself to be an unimportant man, not very clever, by no means brave, protected by his abject fear from any suspicion of treachery, a mere insect in fact, but useful, for a time, so likely to be tolerated. He steeled himself for the great effort of mounting the stair that rose before him, carved from the living rock.

The turret room was in darkness, the air heavy with a fragrance that could not wholly conceal a less pleasant odour of decay. The atmosphere was close, almost stifling.

– Close the door, a voice breathed.

– I must have light, said the man pathetically. I cannot see.

– Stand still until yours eyes adjust. It is not wholly dark.

The man stood for what seemed a long time. The only sound in the room, apart from the thud of his own heart, which seemed very loud to him, was a hoarse, slow breathing, punctuated by the sputter and hiss of what he took to be an incense-burner. Gradually the utter blackness gave way to a brown murk, in which he could make out the shapes of what was in the room; finally he could see well enough to discern the great mass of a man propped up among cushions in the middle of the floor. He advanced towards him and knelt at his side, opening his bag.

– I need to travel, the voice breathed.

– Far?

– Bucharest. Istanbul, perhaps.

– I wouldn't advise it.

– I didn't ask you for advice. Can you make it possible?

– At a cost.

A rumble from the seated man made him correct himself hastily.

– To your health, I meant. Whatever I do to arrest the – ah – process will accelerate it later.

– How long can you give me?

– That depends. The greater the physical demands you make, the shorter the time and the severer the reaction. If you are content with a wheelchair then I could guarantee a fortnight, maybe a month. The stress of travelling is hard to calculate.

– So short a time, said the seated man, but as he seemed to be speaking to himself, the other made no reply.

– This reaction – what form will it take?

– Again, that depends. You have a choice between mind

and body. The body might be sustained for an indefinite time at the expense of mental function. If you wish to keep your mind unimpaired then the body will fail more rapidly, so the mind will go too in the end, or at least your faculties will fail you – speech first, then sight. Your hearing should be last to go.

– Could I write?

– I doubt it: creeping paralysis will be the first symptom of reaction, with a general loss of feeling in the limbs.

– But my mind would remain clear to the last?

The man shrugged.

– I think so. This goes beyond the limits of my knowledge. All I can do is borrow time, at the expense of something else.

The seated man made a curious rasping sound that might have been laughter.

– Don't talk to me about borrowing time. I must travel, and my mind must remain clear. Do whatever is necessary for that and you will be well rewarded.

For a time the doctor busied himself with the contents of his bag, aided by a small pen torch. He drew up a number of syringes, made various injections; his patient sat impassive as a statue throughout. The doctor forced himself to concentrate on what he was doing, not for fear of doing it wrong, but of letting his mind wander – once before in doing this the thought had come to him that his monstrous patient was at his mercy, that by a simple switch of syringes he could free himself from this terrifying bondage; but no sooner had the idea formed than he found himself paralysed, then visited by an excruciating cramp that slowly bent him double. As he writhed on the floor, a voice that seemed inside his head whispered, *I can hear what you are thinking*. Since then, he had been careful to keep his mind wholly on the task in hand.

When the round of injections was complete, the doctor stowed his gear in his bag as slowly as he could, though every nerve in his body was straining to get him out of that room, away from this accursed tower. After what seemed an age, he stood up to take his leave, backing awkwardly towards the door, his stomach in turmoil: it was all he could do to stop himself from running headlong. In the doorway he found that he was unable to move.

– Wait, whispered the voice. I did not say you could go. Further service is required of you.

He opened his mouth to plead, but no words came. His body no longer obeyed his will: with no motivation on his part, he felt himself turn and lurch heavily back into the room.

At dusk a huge old-fashioned car swept through the village lower down the valley, laying down behind it a blanket of blue-grey smoke. Its sombre hue and curtained rear compartment gave it a more than passing resemblance to a hearse. The beam of its enormous headlights betrayed its coming a long way off, and by the time it reached the village all the houses were shuttered and dark: no one lingered outside as the big car passed by, with a curious rhythmic hissing. It squeezed over the little bridge with a grating sound as its long chassis grounded briefly on the crown of the arch, sending out a shower of sparks, then went on down the valley, its single red tail-light glowing like a malevolent eye.

5
What to do about Stephen?

Gerald De Havilland stood at the head of the moonlit stair. On the landing below the murderous angelic children watched him from the wall, curious to see what he would do next. He drew his borrowed dressing gown about him (it was very cold out here, away from his stuffy overheated bedroom) and descended stealthily. On the landing he paused before the portrait, feeling some acknowledgment was due to the ancestral guardians of the family treasure he was on his way to steal. Then he turned his back on them resolutely and carefully made his way down to the hall. At the foot of the stair a gigantic bear reared up on its hind legs, glass eyes glinting in the moonlight. He gave its flank an affectionate pat and sidled past, thankful for the tiled floor on which his slippers made no sound at all.

The door in the panelling was not locked: he opened it with care, but could not prevent a slight creak as he did so. He stood immobile, breath held, ears straining: nothing. He stepped into the room and stood for a full minute, trying to accustom his eyes to the dark, but the shutters were closed and he could not see his hand in front of his face. He felt for his pen torch and turned it on: its slender beam cut through the dark, picking out a patch of walnut sideboard. With deliberate slowness he raised the beam, sliding the patch of light up over the door of the sideboard until he reached the ornate moulding at the top – then he flicked it to the side, and there it was.

The Prince had not replaced the velvet cloth, which lay folded carefully alongside the shabby red box. De Havilland, dry-mouthed, recalled that the box had not been locked before – was it too much to hope that it had been left that way?

He measured with his eye the distance between himself and the red box – fifteen, maybe twenty strides? To be so close – the moment earlier in the day came back to him, with hallucinatory vividness, when the Prince had bent over the Stone and with two deft twists had removed from either end the delicate golden hands: they were exquisite pieces of work, made, as the Prince explained, by a jeweller who had gone on to win fame in the service of the Czar; but De Havilland had no eye for their beauty – instead, all his attention was fixed on the flaws in the Stone that the golden hands had been commissioned to conceal – two indentations that he knew would exactly match the two metal cones at the vacant heart of the Alchemist's Machine.

He had come all this way in a hopeful search for plans, only to stumble on the thing itself – the Stone of Sorrow, the missing piece of the Alchemist's Machine.

He crossed swiftly to the sideboard, flicked open the

catches and opened the box: the thin beam of his torch played upon the Stone, waking sparks of fire in its crystal depths. After a moment's admiration, he gathered it up and slipped it into the pocket of his dressing gown. Then he turned, and there in the doorway were Maurice and the Prince.

He woke with a start, heart thudding, in the familiar surroundings of Silk House. His travel bags, still unopened, lay by the armchair where he had fallen asleep. Outside, it was still daylight. He stood up and stretched, reflecting ruefully that he was getting too old for all this travelling. The sense of alarm engendered by his dream gave way to relief – he had not, in reality, gone farther than the head of the stair, where he had stood a long time in silent communion with the sinister angels, pondering the choices before him, before turning back to his room, where he had lain a long time on his bed, unable to sleep.

The dream was right, of course – he would most certainly have been caught had he been so rash as to make the attempt; but all the same, it pained him to have to turn back with the Stone so nearly within his grasp. Now he would tamely report back to Stephen, who in due course would gather up his cheque book, cross over to Paris (perhaps graciously allowing Gerald De Havilland to tag along) and buy the Stone – and with that purchase would disappear, as far as De Havilland could see, any hope he had of an independent future.

Romantic though he was in other matters, Gerald De Havilland had never given much credence to the notion that the Alchemist's Machine might be the fabled Philosopher's Stone or some such mysterious device of great power – for him, its only value was the price it might fetch, of which he reckoned he could claim a quarter, and might hope for half, since Helen had more than enough money coming to her and had made plain that she wanted nothing to do with the Machine, which she abhorred.

The chief obstacle to any sale was Stephen Langton. That the hugely wealthy Langton had no interest in selling, Gerald De Havilland had always known; but he had hoped he might grow bored with his latest acquisition and soon be persuaded to dispose of it. It was only lately that he had realised how much stronger than mere curiosity were Langton's reasons for retaining the machine.

One night after dinner, Langton had begun to lecture him about "the true nature of alchemy" with a solemnity that made him smile. It wasn't just about making gold from lead, it was much more interesting than *that* (there speaks the rich man, thought De Havilland) – the base metal that was to be transmuted was ourselves, our base human nature, which through the agency of alchemy could be transformed into something near-divine. "That's what the old Garden of Eden story's *really* about – nothing to do with stealing apples: the forbidden fruit is from the Tree of Knowledge; once they eat that, God is afraid that they will eat of the Tree of Life also, and live forever, so he banishes them. Alchemy identifies the Tree of Knowledge with the Philosopher's Stone, and the Tree of Life with the *Elixir Vitae* – the elixir of life."

Even then, he had not caught on – it was only gradually that the true nature of Stephen's interest dawned on him, as he began to piece together from various sources the chronology of Stephen's life. He had long suspected that he was older than he looked, probably nearer seventy than the sprightly sixty he would pass for: but it came as a shock to realise that he must in fact be nearer ninety. Then, of course, it all fell into place: Stephen wanted the Alchemist's Machine as a stepping stone to the one thing all his money could not buy – a way to postpone death indefinitely: the *Elixir Vitae*.

And what that meant, in practical terms, was that he was never likely to give it up – he would buy the Stone, and when that did not work, there would be something else to find – Stephen would go to his grave still looking for the vital missing element, and for as long as that took, Gerald De Havilland would be forced to tag along, with no hope of realizing his share of the Alchemist's Machine in hard cash. But if he had the Stone for himself, then he could sell it to Stephen (through an intermediary of course) for many times what it would cost to buy at auction, where to the outside eye it would be merely a curious crystal with an interesting family history (he had ascertained that the golden hands, whose value was much easier to establish, were to be sold separately). The only problem (now that he had missed the chance of acquiring the Stone for nothing) was raising the cash for the initial purchase...

The sonorous ringing of the doorbell drew him from his reverie.

The man on the doorstep was small, with a scrubby brown beard: something in the way he was dressed suggested that he was foreign. An evangelist for some obscure religious cult? There was no telltale clutch of tracts in his hand, and he seemed to have no bag to carry them in. He had the cringing, beaten air that some beggars have, but without the accompanying signs of neglect and poverty; De Havilland guessed from experience that he was a go-between, and a reluctant one at that. He had an odd manner of cocking his head as if listening to someone at his shoulder; when he did that, his eyes took on a fearful, hunted look.

– Well? what can I do for you?

– I have a proposal to make, Mister Langton.

Gerald De Havilland had long schooled himself not to show surprise, and also to take advantage of whatever opportunity might present itself. He inclined his head, giving the matter his consideration, then said,

– You had best come in.

He showed him into the sitting room, where the little man perched himself on the very edge of the sofa.

– May I offer you something? Tea, coffee?

The little man shook his head.

– What is the nature of this proposal, Mr. – er?

– Doctor. I am Dr. Sarden Negulescu.

He seemed to be trying to convince himself, not wholly successfully.

– My proposition is a financial one.

– You wish me to give you money for some cause?

– No, no! The little doctor waved his hand. You have an article that I wish to buy – for someone else, that is – I am only an agent in this matter.

– And the name of your principal?

The doctor looked uncertain, not understanding the term.

– Your principal: the person you are acting for.

– Ah, yes – my principal –

Again he cocked his head, as if listening. Must be wired for sound, thought De Havilland.

– I cannot name him now. If you would hear the proposal, then perhaps – ?

– Very well. Tell me what you want.

– Some time ago, last summer I think, Mister Langton, you recovered an article of some antiquity from the wreck of a house in France.

– Did I now? And what was the nature of this article that I am supposed to have recovered?

– I think I need not to describe it to you.

Because you don't know, do you, my little man, thought De Havilland. You haven't been told that.

– And for this article which you say I have and will not describe, what are you prepared to offer me?

– One quarter of a million dollars.

De Havilland received the bid impassively, well schooled in this kind of dealing; but his mind raced, calculating the possibilities that had just opened up for him.

– Pounds.

The doctor looked comically uncomprehending.

– I am an old-fashioned man, Dr. Negulescu. I like to reckon in pounds sterling. We are in Britain after all.

– Quarter of a million dollars in pounds? What is that?

– Shall we say five hundred thousand?

– Five hundred thousand dollars? Said the little man, perplexed.

– Call it five hundred thousand pounds, and it's a deal.

No harm in trying, thought De Havilland. How far has your principal authorized you to go? The Doctor's eyes were glazed with concentration as he tried to work out the sum. At last he said, with great deliberation,

– You would be willing to sell for five hundred thousand British pounds sterling?

Damn, should have said a million, thought De Havilland.

– You haven't said what you want to buy yet, and I

haven't said I've got it, but five hundred thousand seems a fair price.

– Please, pleaded the little man, you sell or not? I think you know what we are talking about.

De Havilland gave him a long, considered look. He would have liked to buy time to think about it, but he was afraid to let the opportunity slip.

– When can you have the money?

Because if it's now, you can take it away with you. The doctor was hearing voices again.

– I will have to collect it. It might take a day or two. I will come back.

Damn, thought De Havilland. Still, I'll work something out.

– Very well, Dr. Negulescu. Are you sure I can't offer you anything to drink before you go?

– I thank you, no. Here is a number where you can contact me.

The little man handed him a card. De Havilland saw him to the door. When he had shut it, De Havilland slumped back against it for support: it felt like he had gone twelve rounds with a tough opponent. Out of his whirling thoughts a single question emerged: if someone was willing to pay half a million for the machine, what would he give for the Stone?

Lagging behind it came another: what was he going to do about Stephen?

6
Court Martial

Helen descended the grand stair in her Aunts' house, wearing a dress carefully chosen to advance her years, diamonds twinkling in each ear, an opal (her birth stone) on a fine chain round her neck. Before the double door of the dining room she paused to draw breath, then went in. The first glance told her all she needed to know; the headmistress had indeed been in touch. Helen's place was set on this side of the enormous table; arrayed down the other, like officers at a court martial, were her five Aunts.

Wilhelmine, Augusta, Sidonie, Christina, Ludmilla: Bill, Gus, Sid, Kit, Lud. Those were the names they used among themselves, but never with Helen, nor she to them: she repeated them now inwardly, to cut them down to size, to give her fortitude. Bill, Gus, Sid, Kit, Lud – or Dul, as they called her behind her back, since she was slow-witted.

– Good evening, Aunts, she said gravely, and took her place.

The Aunts nodded and murmured. The first course was brought, and consumed in silence; likewise the second. Helen was not unnerved: it was her Aunts' custom to dine so. Whether that was because they thought dinner table conversation frivolous, or had simply run out of things to say, Helen did not know. She used to think they did it particularly to oppress her, but one day (banished to her room for some misdemeanour) she had crept out to spy on them from the gallery, and there they were, all five of them, eating away, as silent as ever.

The meal went forward at a snail's pace, and Helen grew increasingly nervous, anticipating what was to come. She ate the food mechanically, not tasting it. I must be calm, I must be calm, she told herself: Bill, Gus, Sid, Kit, Lud, she repeated, in descending order of age; then back up again, like a scale: Lud, Kit, Sid, Gus, Bill. The mannish pet names must once have been humorously inappropriate: apart from Lud, who was thick-bodied and short, the Aunts were tall, rangy women, with striking good looks in their youth: now they were handsome still, but their looks had hardened with time, acquiring a masculine severity which made the names more apt than not.

It was only when the last course had been cleared away that the proceedings began.

– Well, Helen, I hear from your school that you have been expelled.

This was Aunt Wilhelmine, the senior Aunt, making the formal opening of hostilities. The others looked at one another, tutting. Helen wondered if they were hearing this for the first time; it would be like Wilhelmine to keep it to herself: she seldom missed an opportunity to assert her position as head of the family.

– I understand it was for violence, continued Aunt Wilhelmine, disdainfully.

– Violence? said the others, in shocked chorus.

– Yes Aunt, said Helen. I punched another girl on the jaw and knocked her out.

– Punched another girl, repeated Aunt Augusta in a whisper. Did you hear that, Sidonie?

– Knocked her out, repeated Sidonie.

Aunt Augusta seemed to be thinking seriously about fainting.

– Well, she is bigger than I am, said Helen reasonably. I didn't want to risk her hitting me back.

Aunt Wilhelmine groaned. The others shook their heads in unison and looked at the table. Aunt Sidonie, the second in command, decided to change the angle of attack.

– I see you brought only one bag. Are you having the rest sent on?

In other words, we expect you to stay here.

– The rest? queried Helen, innocently.

– Your uniform, your school things.

– I'm afraid I threw my uniform out the window of the train.

This produced the effect Helen had hoped for: silence fell; eyes bulged; looks were exchanged.

– You-are-a-profligate-child, said Aunt Christina through gritted teeth.

– It's all right, Aunt Kit, I left the name tags on, so I expect they'll get back to me eventually.

More looks of horror. She could sense the heavy artillery being brought into position.

– It goes without saying that we are very disappointed in you, Helen, said Aunt Wilhelmine.

She dabbed the corners of her mouth with her napkin to indicate her distress.

– And I am sorry indeed to have to say so –

Here it comes, thought Helen.

– But you are behaving exactly like your mother.

– Exactly like your mother, said the others, in supporting chorus.

Helen shook her head regretfully, looking at the table.

– And I had thought we were so different. She's fair, I'm dark –

– I think we're talking about character, Helen, not appearance, Aunt Christina chipped in, helpfully.

Helen looked up, surveying her Aunts with exaggerated care.

– Character? But surely we're very different there? After all, I'm an only child – she had five spiteful older sisters to contend with. They bullied her and made her life a misery until she ran away from them.

There was a collective intake of breath all the way along the other side of the table: again eyes bulged, mouths worked. At the far end, Aunt Ludmilla stirred and began to get up.

– But I haven't run away, said Helen, and you won't bully me.

– Helen, you will go to your room at once, spluttered Aunt Wilhelmine, at once, do you hear?

– No, Aunt, I shall go to my room when I please.

Aunt Ludmilla was on her feet now, her stocky frame bristling. She was intent on coming round to Helen's side of the table, but it was such an absurd size that she could not do it as quickly as she might have wished. Helen remained seated, observing her approach. Aunt Ludmilla, lacking her sisters' wit and sharpness of tongue, favoured more physical

64

methods of control. The last time she had tried them on Helen, when she was eight, Helen had bitten her hand so badly she needed medical attention. There had been repercussions, of course, and Helen had been banished to a spare room, under strict privations, "until she showed herself fit to rejoin civilized society," as Aunt Wilhelmine put it; but Ludmilla had never been left in charge of her again. Often since, Helen had caught a look on her Aunt's face that made it plain she still itched to settle the score.

When she was within a few strides, hand already raised at her side, Helen stood up, and took a step towards her. It was a simple gesture, but its effect was profound. Aunt Ludmilla faltered, suddenly uncertain: she found herself looking up at her niece, seeing her with new eyes: a well-made young woman, who overtopped her by a head; one that had been expelled from school for knocking someone out.

– Don't even think of it, Aunt Lud. I'm not eight years old now. Go and sit down.

Helen held her Aunt's gaze steadily, unflinching. Aunt Ludmilla seemed to deflate; she let her hand fall to her side. It was clear she did not want to climb down as far as obeying her niece, but was at a loss what else to do.

– Don't be an ass, Ludmilla, Aunt Sidonie intervened. Come back here. There are better ways to deal with this. Young lady, I can see we are going to have to stop your allowance for a time.

Ah, money! A so much subtler weapon than any Aunt Ludmilla commanded. Although Wilhelmine was the eldest, it was Sidonie who controlled the purse strings. She was looking at Helen now over her glasses, lips pursed in triumph, just as she did at the bridge table when she played a winning card. The four older sisters played bridge regularly: Ludmilla, however, could never master the game, so it was always Helen who played if one of the others was absent. Her Aunts were skilled players, but Helen could match them. She looked straight back at Aunt Sidonie and said,

– If you attempt to alter the conditions of the trust, I will take you to court.

– You wouldn't dare! spluttered Aunt Christina.

– Try me, said Helen coolly. I have a lawyer already briefed.

This was a lie, a spontaneous fabrication worthy of her father, and from its effect, an inspired invention. Aunts Wilhelmine and Sidonie exchanged speaking looks: they were the brains of the outfit. She knew what they were thinking, just as though she could read their minds. A court case would mean publicity: the news that the heiress to one of the largest family fortunes in Europe was suing her guardians would draw press attention round the world. If there was one thing her Aunts abhorred more than any other (and the list of things they found abhorrent was a lengthy one) it was the unspeakable vulgarity of publicity. Aunt Wilhelmine and Aunt Sidonie were looking at her now, and the expression on their faces told her everything. She had won the decisive trick: they had no cards left to counter her. The subservience of childhood was over: from now on, they would meet as equals.

– I will go to my room now, said Helen. And in the morning I will discuss my future plans with you, Aunt Wilhelmine.

It had been a last moment decision, to leave out Aunt Sidonie – till the words came out of her mouth, she had meant to include her. But she saw at once that her instinct was right: she would not let herself be outnumbered, and it was wise to allow Aunt Wilhelmine her place as head of the family, to elevate and isolate her at the same time. When she reached the door, she turned. The Aunts were sitting as she had left them, ranged along one side of the table, as immobile as exhibits in a museum.

    – Good night, Aunts.

    She went up the stairs three at a time.

7
The Blue Book

In her bedroom, Helen felt too exhilarated to sleep. She climbed into her bed, then got out again and went to sit on the windowsill; but a moment later she stood up again, and went ranging about the room. I need something to read, she thought, something to distract me. There was a substantial shelf of books beside her bed, but somehow none of them appealed. Instead she went to the wardrobe and fished out her bag. She had the oddest sensation of detachment, as though she were standing to one side watching herself. What am I looking in there for? she wondered. All there is are those magazines I bought for the train –

But there was something: a hard flat outline in the outside pocket – what could that be? Of course – Sophie's farewell gift: she had forgotten all about it. She hadn't really felt like chocolates on the train; didn't really feel like them now, either – still, maybe it was something else. She took the package out, climbed onto her bed and arranged a pillow at her back so that she sat against the headboard; the present lay in her lap. She stared at it for a while, wondering what it might be; a strange languor overtook her – a reaction to the earlier excitements perhaps – and she felt her eyelids beginning to droop.

Well, am I going to open it or not? she asked herself. At this rate she would nod off before she got around to it. She made her fingers tear off the paper, deliberately not looking as she did so; what emerged under her hand was something with a covering that was soft, yet resilient; pleasing to the touch. She felt she should recognize what it was, but could not place it. Looking down, she saw that it was a book, bound in fine dark-blue leather. She was immediately delighted, and touched. She had inherited her father's love of old things, and old books especially; she could tell by both the look and the feel of this one that it was certainly very old, probably very valuable. She wondered if Sophie had stolen it from someone else, making up for one theft with another; it was the quirky sort of thing she might do.

There was no title, either on the cover or the spine; the edges of the pages had an uneven, handmade look. She opened the cover and was surprised to find that the text started at once, with no title page or anything like that; the typeface was not one that she recognized – it looked old-fashioned, but was surprisingly clear and legible, except that she could not at all make out the language it was written in. There was something odd about the pages: she felt sure the book was very old, but they had the look of having been freshly printed. Dreamily, she passed her hand over the page, feeling the soft, creamy paper under her fingertips. As she touched the print, she was aware of a slight but perceptible shock: not unpleasant, more a tingle than anything. It was an odd thing, but Helen barely heeded it, because at just the same time, a picture came into her mind, of remarkable vividness and clarity: a large, austere room, stone-flagged and sparsely furnished, with in the middle a big bare table and, studying at it, amid piles of books, a boy. The impression was instantaneous and startling, so that Helen instinctively drew her fingers away; the impression disappeared. Experimentally, she returned her fingers to the page: there was no shock this time, but the picture returned. By way of verification, she lifted her fingers: the words came into focus before her eyes, as impenetrable as before; touching the page again in the same place, she restored the scene. Although some part of her recognized that this was strange, her overriding feeling was delight. Perhaps if she had been wide awake she would have been more curious; but as it was, she felt on the very borderland of sleep, almost slipping into a dream.

She ran her fingers slowly down the page, and was not surprised to find that the scene developed and altered as she did so. She took it for granted that what she was seeing was what the words on the page described.

The boy at the table looked about nine or ten – he was very slight in build – but Helen felt he was older. In the odd way of dreams she managed to be both a spectator – seeing the boy in the room – and in some sense the boy himself. She knew that he was unusually clever and that this room where he was studying was not in his home but in someone else's – a rich man's – where he was allowed to go because of his cleverness. What she sensed most from the boy was an inner strength not hinted at by his external appearance. His meagre frame seemed to conceal an engine of immense power: she had an impression of enormous will. When he looked up from the page she saw that his eyes were extraordinarily light in colour, beyond the lightest grey, almost clear, like diamonds.

Then she saw something quite different – a marvellous city on a headland, gleaming white and golden in the sun, with boats sailing to and fro on glittering waters. She knew this city was what the boy was thinking of, what he had been reading about, and she heard herself say its name: *Byzantium.*

Now she was outside, on the edge of a grassy dell in a rolling sunlit countryside that reminded her powerfully of Scotland, where Jake lived. She could hear sheep bleating somewhere close at hand; the air was mild and fragrant. A girl was walking across the grass to where the boy stood. He looked older now and taller, but still remarkably thin. His gaunt face shone, lit from within, but it was not because of the girl – Helen saw in her face that she knew this, and wished it otherwise. She was simply dressed, with long dark hair and grave, sad eyes.

– And so you are going away, Michael? To Paris?

She was not sure if she heard the words or said them herself, in a strange, thick accent, undoubtedly Scots. The girl held out her hands, the boy took them in his: for a moment it seemed to Helen that it was her hands he held. She felt too the question that the girl had left unasked, because she knew the answer already: *and when will you come back?*

Now she was in another place, at another time: September in a city on an island like a great ship in the middle of a swift river, anchored to either bank by numerous bridges, some built up with houses, like the *Ponte Vecchio* in Florence.

The streets were narrow, overhung with strange, top-heavy houses that seemed to lean towards one another so that the way below was like a tunnel swarming with people, who spilled out into the open spaces before the great cathedral – Notre Dame de Paris. Among the crowds a young man in a leather jerkin made his way, a knapsack on his shoulder, a tall staff in his hand that might have been his brother, so thin were they both. She followed him through the teeming streets until he came at last to a doorway in a filthy lane and entering went up a dark and narrow winding stair.

In a room at the top of the house an old man was working at a long bench, grinding something with a pestle and mortar. He was attended by a grave-faced boy of ten or twelve who between fetching and carrying for his master stood by and watched him reverently with huge dark eyes. The room was furnished from floor to ceiling with books, and more stood in piles on the uneven floor. In the corner was a little truckle bed: she guessed the page boy slept there. A fire burned in the grate beneath a soot-blackened pot hung from chains in the hearth. A window at the far end of the room was open, with shutters turned back, but even so a candle burned at the other end where the man was working. It lit his face from the side, leaving half in shadow, lending the other half a golden tint. It was a cunning face, but not unkind, and steeped in ancient wisdom. He smiled on the young man, with genuine, unexpected warmth. Already he is charmed by him, thought Helen. It was clear that this was the master, the thin young man his pupil – but there was something more between them: a kind of complicity, as at a secret shared. What had he come there to learn?

The young man came often to the high room to work with the old one, now at his bench, now reading under his direction. Helen sensed the bond between the two men grow: gratitude and appreciation on the young one's part, affection and a growing respect for his pupil's abilities from the old one. Yet there was something more – a complex undercurrent of deception: each seemed to be concealing something from the other: while the young one was busy at his tasks, the old man eyed him with a calculating look; when the old man's attention was elsewhere, the young man's hand sought books other than the ones he was set to read, which he perused covertly. There was a sense of climax, of mounting tension, as of some critical time approaching. Always in the background, seeming unnoticed by either of them, the solemn-faced page was in attendance, going to and fro at his master's bidding, yet never uttering a word.

Now it seemed the young man visited the high room secretly, making his way stealthily up the darkened stair when the old man was elsewhere, and the page boy lay asleep on his little bed – on entering, the young man would bend over his sleeping form, muttering under his breath and sprinkling his face with some fine smoke-like powder. Then he would sit long hours, poring over certain volumes by the light of a candle, volumes he was always careful to replace just as they had been, taking pains to conceal any sign of disturbance. Throughout all this, the page boy never stirred, yet now and then the reader would cease his study and look at him, a keen look, tinged with pity.

Now when master and pupil were together, the old man spoke of a great test approaching, the final step by which his student might gain access to the wisdom of the ages: a solemn ritual that must be carefully prepared. The page boy looked on, wide-eyed and awestruck.

On a dark and sleety afternoon, the thin young man

came again to the doorway in the filthy lane, wrapped in a cloak against the cold, carrying his knapsack and his staff – these are all his worldly possessions, thought Helen. There was something in his manner as he mounted the stair that marked this off from any previous occasion: he had the air of someone on the verge of a momentous act. In the room, the air was thick with pungent fragrances: the fire burned with unusual flames of blue-green and red. The floor was clear of books, save one that stood on a lectern in the middle, between two candles; on the floor was drawn a wide circle, inscribed with a complicated pattern of lines and symbols.

– The shutters, Michael, and then approach me here.

The old man positioned himself in the middle of the circle, tracing its patterns with a long staff he held in his hand, while with the other he turned the pages of the book – which made Helen realise that the page boy, who would normally have done that, was not there. It struck her also that the old man was different in some way – perhaps it was just the weird flaring light, but his face seemed somehow smoother, less lined – younger, in fact: *charged with extra life.* And what was that in the corner, humped beneath a sheet?

The young man stood a moment at the window, looking out: it was a dark afternoon. Great flakes of snow began to drift from the leaden sky; the bells of the great cathedral boomed distantly. It is Christmas day, thought Helen. The young man closed the shutters.

The old man's eyes glittered in the gloom.

– Come to me, my son in spirit, come to me and put on wisdom.

There was a deep groaning which seemed to come from under the floor and the fire burned low and dim; the candles flared up an instant, then went out. In that moment Helen saw on the old man's face a sudden change of expression: a look of triumph giving way to astonishment and dismay. A voice – which she knew to be the young man's – whispered, for her ear alone:

Like one that comes, he thinks, by secret and by treacherous paths to seize a citadel, only to find it armed against his coming, and himself made prisoner.

There was a sense of titanic struggle, and it seemed that the room had opened out to a space of cosmic vastness where gigantic forces contended, without limit of time; now it shrank again, as though two ants fought under a walnut shell. The struggle went on almost forever, but at last there was peace, and only darkness.

Then a hand pulled back the shutter, and light streamed into the room. The thin young man looked once more on the world outside, his strange pale eyes steady and unblinking in the sunshine: it was Spring.

Helen's head jerked back and she opened her eyes: I must be nodding off, she thought. She closed the book in her lap and slid it under her pillow, then slipped in under the quilt, enjoying the coolness of the fresh linen. She closed her eyes to resume her sleep: she had the impression of having already dreamed vividly, but of what, she could not recall.

8
An Appointment with the Doctor

Like giant ivory serpents the Eurostar trains lay curved along
the platforms of Waterloo International Station, under the
barrel-vaulted roof striped in alternate light and shade.
Gerald De Havilland stood under the destination board,
contemplating. It was always so much easier to make a
decision to move on in a place like this, where just standing
in the concourse you could feel the tug of all the destinations
that lay at the other end of the line: from here, he could go to
the heart of mainland Europe; from there, to the ends of the
earth.

At the booking office he asked for a ticket to Paris.

– Single or return, sir? said the pretty, oriental-looking
girl at the window.

– Single, please, he said.

That's it, he thought, walking away. Now I've committed
myself, even though it's all still to do – that's the step off the
precipice: no going back now.

On Westminster Bridge he paused, conscious of making it a farewell look. Below him on the river a long glass-roofed riverboat was taking on passengers from a T-shaped jetty; another very like it was just emerging from beneath the bridge. Doubtless the tour guide was drawing the passengers' gaze to the great wheel of the London Eye on their right, revolving so slowly that you would think it stationary. Further downstream the curious curve of the Millennium footbridge allowed the tourists who had seen St. Paul's to cross the river and swap places with those who had done Tate Modern. It was a beautiful day. He took the mobile phone from his pocket, hesitated, then put it back.

He hoped he had made the right move: he was a proficient chess player, but he knew his weaknesses – deep strategy always undid him; Helen, from a frighteningly early age, generally beat him in the long game. But his short game was good: guessing what his opponent was about to do was what he did best. Thus, as soon as he had given the little doctor time to clear Silk House, Gerald De Havilland departed himself, without unpacking his bags (though he took care to pack an additional one). He had dealt long enough at the unconventional end of the business spectrum to know that a deal was only a deal until you could make a better arrangement; from the doctor's point of view, the better arrangement here would be to return that night, probably with some assistance, and take the Machine by force, so saving his principal a tidy sum. As long as he remained at Silk House, he was a sitting duck.

No, the only place to make this sort of deal with any hope of success was at some public rendezvous arranged a short time in advance, with the escape route already prepared – since if the buyer found himself compelled to honour the deal, and actually part with the cash, he would still reserve the right to recover it afterwards should the opportunity present itself. No: in and out quick, then get well away – that was the only way to do it. He was in St. James's Park now; he sat down, waiting for a sign. A little way in front of him were some pelicans, conferring about the wisdom of having a dip. The ruff of feathers at the back of their heads and portly, dignified gait gave them a distinctly professorial air: a band of Oxford dons come up to London on the spree. If they go in, he thought, I'll do it then. Their colloquy continued for some time until one turned abruptly and launched himself from the bank, an initial flurry of water giving way to a stately glide. One after another, his companions followed, moving gracefully across the glittering water. De Havilland took a card from his wallet, took out the phone, and punched in the number.

The call concluded, he headed for Camden Town, made a brief visit to his flat, then retired to the pub across the road. He ordered a pint of Guinness and selected a remote corner table away from the bar that commanded a good view of the door. He settled down to wait. The bar was quiet, almost empty. After a time two old women came in, exchanging chaff with the barman before retiring to a table with what looked like ports-and-peppermint. They were followed by a young man, very smartly dressed, who disappeared behind a newspaper after ordering his drink. Traffic sounds came in from an open window: the clatter of an idling cab; the rumble of a bus; the crackling exhaust of a sports car – a V8 by the sound of it – pulling up at the kerb outside. A door slammed; the engine idled for a time, its throaty throb quite distinct from the other noises; then it revved up and accelerated away into the traffic.

De Havilland looked up and saw that the little doctor had entered the pub. He stood just inside the doorway, gazing about him with the same air of foreignness that De Havilland had remarked at Silk House. He looked so small, so out of place and vulnerable, that any notion of his pulling a double-cross receded to improbability. De Havilland stood and gestured to him to come across. He saw that he was carrying a coat, and beneath it, half-concealed, a bright metal attaché-case of the sort favoured by photographers. The little man approached warily, looking about him like a bad actor expecting an ambush.

– Drink? asked De Havilland, indicating his own.

– Eh – no, said the little man, jerking his hand to his ear. Or yes, if you please.

– What will you have?

The little man goggled uncomprehendingly, his right hand again straying to his ear.

– To drink?

– I – eh – whatever you are having, said the little doctor, desperately.

De Havilland went to the bar, smiling, and ordered a pint of Guinness for the doctor and a half to top up his own. He must still be wearing a wire, he thought, and some sort of earpiece. I wonder where his principal is? Out in the street somewhere, probably: these things had a fairly short operating range. I'll have a look for him when we go out. He'll be in a van, maybe, or more likely a limousine with blackened glass – a rich man with his toys. Typical – gets someone else to do his dirty work, but doesn't trust him to do it properly. Could that mean they were planning a heist to get the money back?

He returned to the table with the drinks.

- You have the money?

The little doctor patted the case, which he had put on the table, but covered (rather theatrically) with his coat.

 - I'll need to see it.

 - You have the goods this time?

 - Not here. Close at hand. We can get them in a minute.

 - You fetch them, please?

Ah, so that's the game: and someone jumps me in the street on the way back, no doubt. No thank you.

 - *We* fetch them, Doc. We'll do this together, if you don't mind.

He stood up. The little man hesitated, then gathered up the case and coat.

 - After you, Doc.

Out on the pavement, the little man stood, looking a little bewildered.

 - Which way, please? I do not know the way.

De Havilland scanned up and down the street, but could see nothing that looked at all out of place.

 - We should –

He broke off: glancing across the road, he had been aware of a light going out that had been on a moment before; though he could not swear to it, he thought it might be in the window of his flat.

 - Walk a little way along the pavement, he said.

He wanted to keep an eye on the window, and on the street door to see if anyone came out, but then a tanker and two buses going by blocked his view. Then a light came on, in the window next to his. Had that been all it was? Probably.

 - We cross the road now, when we can.

It was some time before a gap in the traffic presented

itself and they hurried across. De Havilland kept looking up and down the street but there was nothing that caught his eye. The pavements were still busy; that made some sort of snatch a bit less likely, he felt, but he would keep his eyes peeled all the same. He walked past the door, watching the doctor carefully, but he showed no sign that he had any idea where they were going. Let's take a little stroll, he thought, once around the block to see if the coast is clear.

   – Please, where are we going? You said it was close at hand.

   – Just being careful, Doc.

He turned down past the kebab shop, keeping an eye out for any odd vehicles. A big maroon Bentley glided past in the dusk and he stood and watched it out of sight.

   – Please, what are you doing? I do not like this.

   – Just a little stroll, Doc, to see how the land lies.

They completed an extensive circuit of the block without turning up anything that struck De Havilland as a likely location for the little man's back-up.

   – What is this? said the doctor querulously, when he spied the pub. Now we are back where we started!

   – Just testing, Doc.

Maybe they're indoors, he thought, in a room somewhere. He did a quick survey of the windows overlooking the street, chiding himself as he did so – you think they'll be hanging out the window with their earphones on? Besides, indoors was good – it made them slower to get off the mark. Unless it's *my* indoors they're in, he thought. They were at the street door now. He made the doctor go ahead of him up the stairs, and once they were at the door to the flat, he gave him the keys so that he could go in first, his hands fully occupied.

– What is this? You play trick?

He was frightened now: no harm in that, thought De Havilland.

– No tricks, Doc. Just precautions.

They went into the hall and he switched on the light. Had someone been here recently? It was impossible to tell.

– The door on the left, Doc. Nice and slow.

He pushed open the other doors as he passed, but there was no one. He joined the Doctor in the living room.

– Well, here we are at last, Doc. I'll show you mine if you show me yours.

– I beg your pardon, please?

– The money, Doc – open the case.

– The goods, you have them?

– They're just here.

He turned away from the doctor, but was careful to watch him in the mirror. What he saw startled him: he had half-expected to see him move for a gun, but instead he leaned forward, hands clutching, in a peculiar, predatory fashion, and as he did, his face seemed to change – it might just have been the way the light fell on it, but for a moment he seemed quite a different man. De Havilland felt a chill spread from the region of his kidneys; he spun round suddenly, causing the doctor to start back, a glazed look in his eye.

– What's up, Doc?

The little man did not seem to get the reference. De Havilland, still watching him carefully, worked at the top of the ornate coffee table, releasing hidden catches so that the centre portion slid aside. From the recess that was revealed, he lifted out a small cloth-wrapped bundle.

– This is what you want, I think.

He opened the cloth to reveal the curious skeletal bronze construction that was the Alchemist's machine, never taking his eyes from the doctor's face. The glazed look had gone, to be replaced by what seemed genuine curiosity. Again he put his hand up to his ear.

    – Please, I may pick it up?

    – Please, I may see the money?

By way of answer, the doctor swung the case up onto the table. De Havilland gestured to him to pick up the machine. He flicked back the catches and opened the lid. The case was neatly packed with bundles of rose-coloured notes, still in their wrappers. He took one out: 100x£50, it said on the wrapper. He fanned through the crisp notes, holding them up to his nose. It looked and smelled like the real thing. He began counting the top layer.

    – Please, it is complete?

    – Well, give me a minute to check – I can't count that fast.

    – No, I mean the machine – it is all here?

    – Well all the parts we found in Ruggiero's house are there, if that's what you mean. We didn't get it ready made, you know, we had to assemble it ourselves, and bloody hard work it was too, I can tell you.

    – It is just that there is a space here, you see?

    – Yes, we noticed that, but as I said, all the parts we found are there. Is that a problem? You offered half-a-million for what we had. Well, that's it.

The hand went up to the ear again; the little man winced.

    – No, no, it is not a problem. I am sure my principal will be quite satisfied.

So how does he know that? De Havilland wondered. He's not been able to see it, to check. He continued his count of the top layer: 33 bundles; 34, with the one he was already holding. He tipped them onto the settee. 33 in the next layer: he emptied that too. And another 33. 100 bundles of £5000 each. It all seemed to be there and in order.

— Well, Doc, it looks like we have a deal.

The little man nodded, wrapping the bronze. De Havilland watched him closely as he placed it in the case. *No last minute tricks, now – don't disappoint me, Doc.*

— I'd offer you something, but I'm sure you'd rather get away –

And I'd certainly rather see the back of you.

— Of course, I must go.

He made his way into the hall, De Havilland following. Just keep going, Doc, right out that door. He opened the door and stepped out, putting his hand up in an automatic gesture to switch out the light. For a moment he was silhouetted against the light on the stair, so that De Havilland could only see the outline of his head as he turned to say, in a quite different voice,

— Goodbye, Mr. De Havilland.

9
Two's Company

On Monday morning, Jake had scarcely been in school five minutes before three separate people told him, with some excitement, that his English teacher had disappeared.

– Macintosh? What do you mean, disappeared?

– Done a runner. He didn't turn up for registration. Mr. Marks is fuming!

Jake was inclined to be sceptical.

– He's probably just slept in. Remember Holligan?

The late, unlamented Mr. Holligan had been a notorious latecomer.

– Don't you believe it! said another boy. He's run off with Miss Wilbright, bet you anything!

Jake laughed scornfully, recalling Miss Wilbright's veiled hints to him on Friday.

– Wilbright and Macintosh! I hardly think so – she can't stand him!

– Not what I heard. Anyway, he's off, she's off – stands

to reason, doesn't it?

Though Jake felt this logic was hardly watertight, he was too preoccupied by his own thoughts to say so. Wilbright and Macintosh both off school; Macintosh at least under some sort of cloud – it could hardly be just coincidence. Maybe... suppose Macintosh was some sort of pervert, and Wilbright knew that, say from teaching in another school (they were both new that session) – then after she had seen him talking to Jake, she might have said something, to warn him off – and now of course she would be explaining that to the education authority, or maybe even the police – it all fitted together.

– Penny for them, Jake?

It was the delectable and ubiquitous Alison Macdonald. Ubiquitous, because she seemed to be everywhere, these days – or at least, everywhere Jake was: chess club, badminton, even the maths revision sessions at lunchtime; and delectable, because, well, she was.

– Eh? O, hi Alison.

– What d'you think of Wilbright and Macintosh then?

– I don't see why everyone's so determined to pair them off – not the likeliest couple, I'd have thought.

– I don't know – opposites attract, maybe. Anyway, Marie Glover saw them out together on Friday night.

– And is Miss Glover's eyesight to be relied upon, do you think, especially on a Friday night?

He said it in the gruff tones of Mr. Marks, the deputy head, and Alison laughed, but Jake was wondering at this latest revelation – Friday night! right after he had seen them – of course, maybe that fitted in with his own theory.

– But it's not just Marie Glover, said Alison, lots of folk have seen them together.

– Just because they were seen together doesn't mean they're going out with one another, said Jake. He paused, then added as an afterthought, I mean look at us...

They were looking at one another as he said it, and the full sense of the words struck them both at the same time: they seemed to spend a long time, just looking at each other, then Alison smiled, very slowly.

– But then again, she said, (her eyes widening) it doesn't mean they're not.

They both smiled at that, still looking at one another.

For the rest of the day, the matter of Miss Wilbright and Mr. Macintosh was the farthest thing from Jake's mind. Next farthest was schoolwork. In class after class, teacher after teacher upbraided him, their words like a song's refrain:

– Giacometti, you're dreaming.

He could not deny it. He was dreaming. Thoughts of Alison spread from the centre of his mind to the outermost periphery, leaving no room for anything else. His life, he felt, had just made a fundamental, critical shift.

When Jake had returned to school after the summer, it was to find that the girlfriend question – i.e. whether you had one or not – had changed from a matter of minor importance to a key social indicator. The immature youth, the mere fledgling boy, roamed still in flocks of his own kind, encountering the opposite sex warily, as one might an alien race, believed to be hostile. The young man, on the other hand, was distinguished by his having a particular female friend, with whom much of his time was spent – though not all, since there were still important matters to discuss with other mature males, such as football.

Jake considered that he had managed this tricky transition rather well: from the outset, he was able to present Helen as his girlfriend, and could back up his claim with photographic evidence of the two of them together in a variety of exotic locations; further, he could allude to a week spent in her company *without adult supervision* – though being a gentleman, he left the actual details to be guessed at. That Helen lived in Switzerland was not the disadvantage it might seem – not only did it confer on her the additional glamour of exotic foreignness, it freed Jake from the more tiresome obligations that seemed to beset those with girlfriends more handily located, such as endless trailing around shops (when he could have been playing football) watching soppy films (instead of proper action movies) and talking, talking, talking. Thus, thanks to Helen, he was able to acquit himself with considerable aplomb in the girlfriend stakes, while retaining complete freedom of action –the best of both worlds.

All this, of course, had been accomplished without informing Helen of her official status as his girlfriend, a point that had given Jake some pangs of conscience, but which now – with the advent of Alison – relieved him of the painful task of telling her she was chucked. Nevertheless, there was still some ritual to be gone through – Helen had been enthroned in his heart too long to be dismissed without ceremony.

[*scene: a misty cliff-top, with gulls mewing piteously, and from below, the melancholy crash of breaking waves. Enter, from the right, Jake, attired as a Naval lieutenant of the Napoleonic period, complete with sword and tricorn hat. He stands at the cliff's edge, gazing pensively seaward. To him, from the left, Helen, in female costume of the same period, complete with Bo-peep hat, which*

*she unties and removes, letting her hair stream in the wind. They
stand awhile in silence, contemplating the sunset.*]

Jake: The sun is setting.
Helen: The day draws to its close.
[*pause*]
Jake: As all things must, in time.
[*Helen, catching a deeper meaning in his words, turns to look at
him; he returns her gaze*]
Jake: We have been through many things together, Helen.
Helen: We have.
Jake: And I shall always treasure your friendship.
Helen: (*stifling a sob*) I had hoped we might be more than
friends.
Jake: You know that cannot be – we live in different worlds.
Helen: O, Jake –
Jake: (*implacably*) It's no use, Helen, you know that our ways
do not lie together – I must make my fortune; yours is made
already.
Helen: (*with an indignant gesture*) I would it were not so!
Jake: (*calmly, his hand raised in admonition*) It is futile to wish
things otherwise. That is your destiny: mine lies elsewhere.
Helen (*weeping silently*) O, Jake! Jake!
Jake (*relenting, his heart touched*) Perhaps, in after years, we
shall meet again.
[*Helen looks at him with sudden hope*]
Jake: As friends.
Helen (*pleading*) Only as friends?
Jake: Always as friends. (*taking her hands, he kisses her tenderly
on the forehead*) Goodbye, Helen.
[*The sun sets*]
A voice: Giacometti, you're dreaming!

Alison was lingering at the gate when school ended.

– Walk you home?

– If you like.

It was a beautiful day. All around him, Jake was aware of the onset of Spring: the cherry trees like pink explosions; everything in bud or just coming into leaf; birds singing. On their homeward journey their talk ranged over divers topics: art, literature, music, history, the future, food, friends, foes, likes and dislikes, parents, families, relatives.

There was one note of discord in this learned and harmonious discourse: the fact that, with the Easter holidays approaching, they would not be able to see one another. Alison, it seemed, was away for the second week; Jake (how he cursed it now, though he had been delighted at the time) had been invited to Silk House for the start of the holidays – in fact (the thought struck him like a thunderclap) he was actually going sooner than that – the day after tomorrow.

– What, you mean you're not even going to be at school for the rest of the week? said Alison reproachfully.

– No, said the wretched Jake.

Why had he wheedled his parents into letting him go early? It was impossible to back out of it now. Still, the invitation was open ended – "come down for a few days," Stephen Langton had said – perhaps he could come back sooner?

– I don't think I can get out of going, but I might be able to cut it short.

Alison brightened. They had by now arrived at Jake's doorstep; had been standing at it for some time in fact.

– Would you like to come in? For a cup of tea, or something?

Alison beamed. She would like that very much.

Jake swung into the hall with his usual shouted greetings, accompanied by the slamming of his school bag into the hallstand. His mother's voice came out in answer from the kitchen, followed shortly by his mother herself, wiping her hands on her apron.

– Hello, son – you've got – O, who's this?

– Hi Mum! This is Alison.

– Hello, Alison, pleased to meet you.

– Hi, Mrs. Giacometti.

– You've got a visitor, Jake.

His mother nodded in the direction of the sitting room; Jake opened the door and went in, Alison at his shoulder.

–Hello, Jake.

It was Helen.

10
What's It All About?

Jake sat across the table from Helen. Outside the window, the platforms of Central Station slid away behind them; now they were travelling through a narrow canyon with walls of soot-blackened stone, now among a great sprawl of houses all the same. There was, as ever on the railway, the sense of passing behind things, seeing their hidden aspects: the backs of houses, untidy with branching drainpipes; back gardens strewn with toys or with washing hanging out or simply overgrown; blank walls of factories; derelict sites. They were going south, to Silk House. They had barely spoken a word since Jake got on the train, coming straight from school, to find Helen already there.

He looked at Helen, gazing fixedly out the window: she might have been travelling alone, and Jake a stranger. Why did she insist on coming if she was going to act like this?

It was all to do with Alison, he supposed. It was the last thing he had expected, to walk into his own living room and find Helen sitting there – and it was clearly the last thing Helen expected, to see him arrive with Alison. *Her face fell:* it was not an expression he had thought much about before, but in that moment, he saw it defined – a kind of collapse, as if all the muscles of her face had suddenly failed – one moment she was smiling, greeting him, the next it all seemed to slip – her mouth fell open, her eyes bulged, everything went slack. It only lasted for a second before she marshalled herself and raised the ghastly semblance of a smile, but it was clear that she had been completely thrown by the turn events had taken.

Well, what did she expect? thought Jake, not without a certain cruel satisfaction. Had she banked on just turning up out of the blue to find him ready and waiting, eager to do her will? That had certainly been her style in the past, when more than once Jake had felt himself little better than an item of baggage that Helen dangled after her – we can do this, go there, stay with my cousin in X, Y or Z – she seemed to have a limitless supply of cousins, one in every major city in Europe. The idea that Jake might actually have some plans of his own, might not wish to fall in with Helen's impulsive schemes, was simply swept aside – as far as Helen was concerned, consultation meant giving the other party the opportunity to agree with her proposal.

Well, now it was different. He had moved on from where she had expected him to be; she was the one floundering after him now. The meeting with Alison had been awkward all round, but he thought he had made it clear enough where he stood, which was (literally) with Alison – he had stayed on her side of the room, sat beside her on the sofa. Helen as ever was able to make light conversation about nothing, but it was clear that she wanted Alison out of the road so she could speak to Jake alone – an opportunity Jake had been careful to avoid giving her. Unfortunately, Alison was obviously none too pleased to find Helen there either, and Jake had felt he had to work hard to placate her, to make it clear that he had nothing at all to do with Helen's being there, but it did not stop him feeling guilty about it, which made him feel angry at Helen – that she should have chosen just that one evening to turn up unannounced! It was the sort of thing that made you think God was a practical joker.

And just why was she there anyway? The account she gave was patently ridiculous – she had just happened to be in Glasgow, and thought she would drop in. How could she just happen to be in Glasgow? She lived in *Switzerland*, for god's sake! And why wasn't she at school, anyway? These posh private schools seemed to have holidays all the time – typical: the more you pay, the less you get. As far as Jake could work out, what must really have happened was that Helen had come north with some scheme in her head that she had just assumed he would fall in with, and she was now so completely thrown by finding things other than she expected them to be that she didn't know what to do – which did make him feel a little sorry for her, but only a little, since her unquestioning assumption that the world would accommodate itself to her will was one of the things that most irritated him about Helen (and, if he was honest, most envied) – to see her experience life as ordinary mortals did was very satisfying, and could do her nothing but good.

She had made a couple of attempts to corner him before dinner, but he had thwarted them, and then at the table it was back to polite meaningless conversation again – it was only when his Mum had started talking about his going to Silk House that her manner had changed again. Her first reaction puzzled Jake, and was still puzzling him now – he had happened to be looking at her when his Mum mentioned the trip to Silk House, and the expression on her face was most peculiar – shock, almost, he would have said – and after that, well, he could have sworn she was afraid of something. But if that was strange enough, what followed was almost bizarre – all of a sudden, her plans (which had been so vague) became crystal clear – Jake was going to Silk House? Why, that was where she was going too (with no mention of how she happened to be going via Glasgow, a detour of about a thousand miles) and wouldn't it make sense for them to go together? Well of course it would, said his parents, with that irritating habit of making decisions on his behalf – and after that, Helen had seemed – well, *relieved* was the nearest word he could think of: she seemed almost happy, and no longer anxious to speak to him alone at all.

Because she knew she'd have me as a captive audience once we were on the train, thought Jake, yet here she was gazing out the window as though he wasn't even there. What on earth was it all about? He supposed most of it must be Alison, but the Silk House bit had to be something separate. They had been there together for a couple of days between Christmas and New Year, and beneath the surface jollity even Jake (who was the first to admit he was not the most perceptive of people) had been aware of a definite tension between Helen's father and Stephen Langton; it had something to do with the Alchemist's Machine, which they had succeeded in reassembling, only to find, of course, that it didn't work. When they had gone out for a walk afterwards, Helen had said to him that her father wanted to sell it and take his share of the profits, but that Stephen Langton wouldn't hear of it.

So was *that* it? There were four of them who could make some sort of claim on the Machine – it was Stephen Langton who had actually found it, but only after Jake and Helen had solved the puzzle in the picture that told them where it was, and of course Helen's father had really started the whole business by stealing the picture in the first place, so they could all claim an equal share – so if Helen's father wanted to sell, and Helen went along with him (which she would, because she had never liked their having the Machine in the first place) and Stephen Langton was against – then that made his, Jake's, the decisive vote: he could make a 3-1 majority to sell, or he could tie it at 2-2, which presumably meant there would be no change and they would keep it. That *must* be it – Helen had come up to persuade him to her father's side, then when she heard he was going to Silk House, she must have feared some sort of conspiracy between him and Stephen Langton – so she decided to tag along in the hope of dissuading him.

Well, and where did he stand? He was not really sure – as the events of the summer had receded, so had his initial conviction that this collection of old bits of metal might really be something very special – the fabulous Philosopher's Stone, no less! It was a disappointment, when Christmas came round, to find that they had put it back together but it did not do anything – a disappointment, but not really a surprise. Only Stephen Langton seemed to retain any real belief in it – he had insisted that there must still be a part missing – and there *was* a sort of space in the middle of it where it might go. There was certainly one part of him sided with Mr. Langton – he did *want* it to be the Philosopher's Stone, but it was a bit like wanting there to be a Loch Ness Monster – it would make life more interesting, but when you came down to it, well, you couldn't really believe it. Did that mean he wanted to sell it, then? There, he could see Gerald De Havilland's point of view – both Mr. Langton and Helen had more money than they knew what to do with already, so selling it would make no real difference to them, but it would to Helen's dad and to him – the only question was, how much was it worth?

Aurelian Pounce had been willing to kill to get it, so clearly it was valuable to him, but that was because he was a dabbler in the occult and black magic and obviously believed it was the Philosopher's Stone or some sort of powerful magical device – presumably there were others like him, but were they exactly the sort of people it was good to do business with? Might they not prefer Pounce's methods – kidnap, torture, murder – to a straightforward cash transaction? Of course it was some sort of antique, and it might well be worth something because of that, if they could auction it, say – but wouldn't there be problems when it came to saying where they had got it from? He did know that "provenance" was an important thing when it came to auctions. So it would have to be a private sale then – but he knew that collectors like Stephen made lots of those, so that wasn't impossible, except that Stephen was the one man who did not want to sell.

Perhaps the best thing would be to wait and see if there was a missing part that they could find – because it would be worth more if it was complete, at any rate, and there was also just that slender possibility that it might – it just *might* – be the Philosopher's Stone after all... so that was his decision, then – he would side with Stephen, at least until they had tried to find if there was a missing part. Pleased to have sorted that out, he returned his attention to Helen.

She was crying.

It was not a noisy performance – instead she sat with quiet dignity, looking straight in front of her, as the tears welled up and spilled over, following one another in the same track over the contours of her face: it was like watching a statue weep.

Jake felt a great surge of pity – he wanted to reach out and stem the flow of her tears, wipe them away – he could not bear to see her cry, to think that he had made her cry – and then he felt a sudden spurt of anger: she was manipulating him, trying to make him feel bad about dumping her! He hardened his heart.

– Look, Helen, there's really no point in crying – you'll get over it. I'm with Alison now – anyway, it's not like we'd ever said we were going out or anything, or even if we ever could, really, with you being in Switzerland –

He faltered to a halt. Helen was looking at him with the strangest expression on her face, a sort of complete disbelief: he couldn't tell if she meant to laugh or cry.

– O, Jake! I don't mind your having a girlfriend – that isn't what it's about at *all*!

– Well, what is it then? asked Jake, mystified.

11
A Step With No Return

Well, where do I begin? I've been expelled from school – but it isn't that – and I've had a big showdown with The Aunts – it isn't that either, because I won – they agreed I didn't have to go back to school and that I could study to be a literary translator – I've decided that's what I want to be – so I said I wanted to got to Cambridge, to see if I could study there, so that I could be near Dad, and they even accepted that as meek as little lambs.

So off I went to London then caught the train to Manorhampton, for Silk House. I was reading Dante – La Vita Nuova, I don't know if you know it? It's a funny sort of book – part of it's an account of his love for Beatrice, but it's also a kind of manual for writing sonnets. Anyway, I thought I might as well practice my translation, if that's what I'm going to do, and there was this one line that stuck in my head – "Io tenni li piedi in quella parte de la vita di là da la quale non si puote ire più per intendimento di ritornare" *which means* "I had set foot in* that part of life beyond which one cannot go with any hope of returning".

That was me, don't you see? I had committed myself, left all these things behind me that I wasn't going back to – school, The Aunts, all that part of my life – and here I was stepping into my future. And then when I arrived at Manorhampton it made me think about it even more, because of course I remembered when you and I came there last summer, and in a way that was really where it all started, because if we'd turned back then none of this would have happened – so you can imagine the kind of things that were going through my head as I scrunched up the drive to Silk House – I'd had the taxi drop me off at the church so I could walk the rest of the way, it was such a lovely afternoon.

Anyway, I was just about to ring the bell – thinking how surprised they'd be to see me – when I noticed the door wasn't properly shut, so I thought I'd just sneak in and surprise them properly.

Do you know what it's like when you step into a place and know right away there's something wrong? You try to shrug it off, pretend it's just your imagination, but of course just by doing that you're already believing it. It took me a bit to work out just what it was – then I realised how quiet it was – I couldn't even hear the clock, you know the big fancy one in the hall that has to be wound every day? I looked at it, and sure enough it had stopped. Nothing too odd about that, of course, because they might just have gone out for the day, except for the door's being open – but maybe they went out in a hurry and didn't close it properly, I told myself.

I nearly went back to close it myself then, because I was thinking of their faces when they came back and found me sitting in the house waiting for them, and how lucky they were that it was me and not a burglar that found the door was open – but then that *stopped me in my tracks, because I suddenly thought that maybe there was a burglar – I was afraid even to breathe – I remember just staring at this shaft of sunlight that was shining across the hall, with all the little bits of dust catching the light, trying to think what to do – and all the time it was just so quiet.*

It was the silence that persuaded me to go on – I was sure that if anyone was there I must have heard him, so I tiptoed to the first room and I saw at once that someone had been there – not that it was a mess or anything, it hadn't been ransacked – it was more like it had been searched very thoroughly and methodically, by someone who was looking for one particular thing – and as soon as I thought that, I knew – I just knew – that whoever it was had been looking for the Alchemist's Machine.

Sure enough, when I went into the next room – remember the one where we set up the projector to show the slide of the painting on the wall? – the bookshelves were swung back and you could see right into the collections room – so whoever it was had known about that, or else had worked it out. In a way, that made me less afraid, because I reckoned that the person must be long gone, because if he had found the collections room, he must have got what he came for.

I stuck my head in, and I saw right away that the little table where the machine used to be – you know, the one with the orange velvet cover – was empty; nothing else was disturbed, although the blinds on all the cabinets were lifted – whoever had come for the machine seemed to have checked to see if there was anything else that took his fancy.

I'm not really sure why I went on searching, but part of me knew that there was still something more to find – so I went across into the next room – you know, the one with the French windows that look onto the garden – and it was there I saw it. I couldn't make out what it was at first, it was like one of those mystery

pictures where you see a familiar object from an unusual angle –
then I realised it was a shoe – what had puzzled me was that it
seemed to be standing on its heel, in a way that just looked
impossible.

I went in a few steps further and saw that there was a man
lying on the floor behind the armchair. I couldn't see his face,
because it was covered with a cloth – there was a small table beside
him that had been upset on the floor, and a vase of flowers – they
were spread out in an arc, almost arranged, but I think what must
have happened was the man had grabbed the cloth as he fell and
pulled the table over.

I suppose I must have been in shock, but I found myself
thinking very calmly that I wouldn't know who it was until I lifted
the cloth – in a way, it was waiting for me to make it happen – back
to Dante again, I suppose – another step with no return. All the
time another part of me was saying, how can you not know who it
is? Because of course I knew that it could be my father, or else
Stephen Langton – or maybe someone else altogether, a complete
stranger – but I really couldn't tell, not at all – I mean Dad and
Stephen are both about the same size, and they don't dress that
differently, and I suppose that you're used to seeing people standing
up, not sprawled flat on their backs.

The last thing in the world I wanted to do was lift that cloth,
but it was the only thing I could do, because of course I had to
know – so I tried to make myself be very calm, and I knelt down
and took it off.

It was Stephen Langton.

I was so relieved that it wasn't my Dad that found I was
smiling – I think I even might have laughed – yet at the same time
I was telling myself I should be feeling bad, that it was Mr. Langton
lying there – only somehow it wasn't him, I mean it was his body,
but it wasn't him – I was in no doubt that he was dead, because

the hilt of a knife was sticking out of his chest – it was black, with what looked like a strip of leather wound round it – funny how you register every little detail. I even remember noticing that there was very little blood on it, and thinking that was because the knife had gone right through him so that it would all come out the back.

I don't think I felt anything – just numb, and so relieved that it wasn't Dad.

I stood up, and someone put a hand over my mouth and another on my neck, pressing it at the side, here – I think it must have been a woman, not so much because of the hands – they were very smooth and cool – but because of the scent, which was the last thing I was aware of before I passed out.

When I came to, I was sitting in an armchair, and this man was looking at me – rather anxiously, I thought. The funny thing was that as soon as I set eyes on him I felt he was someone I'd seen before, but I just can't place him. When he saw that I was awake, he asked if I was all right – he thought I must have fainted, because he found me lying on the floor when he came in. He said his name was Raeburn – Macintosh Raeburn – which rang a bell, but not because of the face – then he said he was writer and that he had an appointment to see Stephen Langton, and I remembered that Stephen had a book by him when we were down at Christmas that he was very interested in – what was it called? The Elixir and the Stone, that was it.

I said I was there to meet my father and I saw him glancing down at the body, so I said "no, that's not him – that's Mr. Langton; my father's not here" and a look passed over his face that told me exactly what he was thinking and I suddenly realised that my father was in deep trouble – not that I think he did it for a minute – why would he? – but because of what everyone else was bound to think. Then Raeburn asked if I had called the police, because if I hadn't, then it might be better if we had never been there at all, because there was really nothing we could do apart from make trouble for ourselves and maybe other people too, by which I knew he meant Dad. So we went out leaving everything just as it was, then I had the bright idea of pulling the door shut – it was on the spring lock – and ringing the bell, so that I could say I had come and found no-one home, then he had turned up – he had a car parked in the drive, a very odd-looking old sports car, apple green, that looked like a fish – it even had fins.

He asked if there was anywhere I wanted to go so I said London – I reckoned I would go to Dad's flat to see if he was there, or if there was any clue to where he might be, though I didn't tell Raeburn that – my main concern was how to get rid of him, because although I wanted to get away from there as quickly as possible and get to London without having to take the train – I thought the fewer people who saw me there, the better – I definitely did not want him hanging around afterwards.

Anyway, I got into the car, and just as we were turning I looked back at the house, and I could have sworn there was someone standing at the side of the window looking out – quite tall and dark, more like a woman than a man, but it was just a fleeting impression – the car was moving and when the angle changed it seemed not to be there any more, so maybe it was just some trick of the light.

Once we were on the road the car was very noisy, which I was grateful for, since I didn't want to talk. Then after a bit Raeburn shouted something and pointed behind us and I turned round and saw a black Maserati. Raeburn seemed to think it was following us but I thought he was just being melodramatic to try and impress me. He had been driving very fast, but now he slowed right down so that the Maserati would have to pass us, but it slowed down as well. "Doesn't want to risk losing us" said Raeburn, though I reckoned the driver might just have decided to stop, maybe to check where he was on the map. When we were round the next corner Raeburn accelerated away really hard, and sure enough when we came to the next straight there was the Maserati coming after us hell-for-leather.

He seemed to be gaining on us, but then we came to a junction—there was a big articulated lorry heading up a long queue of traffic on the main road, and Raeburn shot right out in front of it – you should have heard the blare of its horns – and the Maserati had to pull up and wait. He drove flat out all the way to London – "just to make sure" – he said – but I reckon he was showing off. I'm still not sure if the Maserati was really following us or not.

In London I had a really smart idea for getting rid of him – I asked him to drop me off at Camden Town tube station, which of course is right next to Dad's flat, but he would think I was going on somewhere else. I did notice that he stayed beside the kerb watching until I actually went into the station and waved good-bye to him, then he shot off with a great crackle of exhausts. I thought I'd best stay in the station for a minute or two just to be on the safe side, and as I turned round someone coming out caught me in the thigh with the corner of a case – it was one of those shiny metal ones, like photographers have, and it was sharp, I can tell you. I gave the man who had it a real dirty look and asked if he was trying to cripple me, but he didn't say anything, just goggled at me – a little man with a scrubby brown beard; I think he was foreign.

So anyway, after a bit I limped out and went up to Dad's flat. I half-hoped he might be in, but it was empty, and as soon as I was inside I just collapsed on the floor and wept and wept – I suppose it was some sort of delayed reaction. After a bit I picked myself up and went to see if there were any clues to Dad's whereabouts. I checked on his computer and saw that a couple of days before he had looked up the Eurostar website, and that he had also been checking out various auction houses in Paris – there were some *notes on the desk with dates and initials. I was starving, but there was no food in the house, so I nipped out to the Turkish restaurant round the corner – they were really pleased when they found I could speak some Turkish, and they gave me all sorts of extra things that didn't appear on the bill – they were really warm and kind, even if the waiter did get a bit carried away and asked me to marry him.*

It was just the thing I needed though, a bit of human kindness, and I went back up to the flat feeling better than I had all day. I was on the landing, looking for the key – I was sure I had put it in my pocket, then it turned up in my purse. I was just about to put it in the lock when I noticed that the hall light was on. I felt pretty sure I hadn't left it on – in fact I couldn't recall having the lights on at all – but on the other hand, I couldn't recall putting the key in my purse either, and I'd done that.

I must have stood for about a minute, like some sort of half-wit, with the key poised just in front of the lock as if I didn't know what to do next – and then I saw the door handle start to turn. I got a terrible fright and I skipped up the stairs out of sight. I could hear the door opening below, and a voice speaking, though I couldn't make out what it said. I almost laughed aloud when the obvious explanation occurred to me – it was Dad, of course! I had just turned to go back down when I heard footsteps coming up to meet me.

I was on the next landing, and when I looked down I saw someone at the turn of the stair below – it was the same man I had seen in the tube station, the foreign-looking one who had crippled me with his brief case. He didn't see me because he was looking back down the stairs with an expression on his face that chilled me to the bone – it was like some sort of animal watching its prey. I panicked and ran up the stairs to the next floor – I think I had some notion of knocking on all the doors until someone let me in – but then I had a horrible vision of the man coming up after me, and finding me pathetically scrabbling to get away from him, with nowhere to go.

I told myself that he hadn't seen me, that I could just be someone from the next floor, or a visitor who had found no one in – all I had to do was walk down the stairs past him, and out – and even if I had to run, at least it would be towards the street. So I steeled myself, took a few deep breaths, and went down. He was still there, lurking at the corner. I've never been so afraid in all my life as I was when I walked down that last flight of steps – my legs felt like rubber. When I was a few steps above him, he looked round – and his eyes! It was horrible – there was a concentrated hatred in them, a sort of hunger. I think I would have been paralysed if he'd given me more than a glance, but he looked away almost at once – he seemed intent on watching the landing below.

I squeezed past him and went down the stairs – it was all I could do to stop myself breaking into a run. All the way down I felt those eyes on my back – I was careful to pass Dad's door without so much as a glance – I was terrified he'd connect me with it somehow and come after me. When I got out onto the street, I couldn't help myself – I did run. I suppose the sensible thing would have been to go to the tube station, but that was where I had seen him first, so instead I just ran and ran through the streets until I saw a bus and jumped on it.

Then I started thinking how I could get as far from London as I could, so I came to you.

12
Roller Coaster

After Helen had finished, Jake found himself unable to speak. Her delivery had been fluent and uninterruptible, a long pent-up force suddenly released; she had spoken in a curiously detached way, her eyes focused on a point a little way in front of her. At several points Jake had tried to intervene – particularly at the revelation that Stephen Langton had been murdered – but now that he was free to speak, he found himself unable to do so.

His feelings came at him from all directions at once: Mr. Langton's death, he knew, ought to be accorded most importance – yet he struggled to think beyond the bare fact: *so Stephen Langton is dead, then* – where were you supposed to go after that? Besides, so many other things crowded in upon him – his shame, or rather embarrassment, at having been so ludicrously wrong about Helen, thinking her jealous of Alison, when that was something that must not even have registered on the scale with her after what she had been through; an unmistakable tingle of excitement (and fear) at having been suddenly drawn out of his safe comfortable world into a tale of murder and intrigue; but more than anything, the words that Helen had concluded with: *so I came to you.*

In all her troubles, it was him she had turned to – instinctively, without questioning that he would be there to help her. And he had come so close to letting her down! A wave of guilt swept over him, followed swiftly by pleasurable feelings of abasement and repentance. He had been disloyal, but now he would be true – indeed, his momentary turning aside allowed him to demonstrate where his real allegiance lay – he had been called back to his allotted destiny; he would sacrifice any thought of Alison (and did so, then and there) and devote himself henceforward exclusively to Helen, his coeval to the minute, his soul twin. He felt a warm glow of affection suffuse him.

– Well I'm going to have a sleep, said Helen, deciding that she had waited long enough for Jake to make some response. Telling the tale had exhausted her: she felt light and hollow, like an empty jug.

Jake watched as Helen rolled her jacket into a pillow and fell almost instantly asleep: it was one of her most endearing traits (but were they not all endearing?) this capacity of hers to fall asleep whenever she felt like it, regardless of where she found herself. Her face in repose had the calm beauty of a classical statue. He sat, a loyal guardian, content just to watch her.

It was fate, he decided. They were clearly meant to be together – their first meeting in Florence had been such pure chance – two people from two entirely different countries meeting up in a third; and now, just at the very point where he had thought to go in another direction (he loyally suppressed the name of Alison) she had appeared again, against all the odds, in the very nick of time. If that wasn't proof of his manifest destiny to be with her, what was?

He must have dozed a little himself: the next thing he was aware of was Helen sitting up, suddenly awake.

– Of course! she said. I *knew* I'd seen him before.

Jake's expression made his puzzlement plain.

– Macintosh Raeburn, the man I met at Silk House. As soon as I saw him, I knew he was familiar, I just couldn't say from where. My gentleman caller!

This did not take Jake much further on the road to comprehension.

– Gentleman caller? he queried.

– That's what The Aunts call them, said Helen with a laugh. Very Tennessee Williams, don't you think?

Jake made a non-committal noise. *Tennessee Williams?* What was she on about? He had not figured Helen for a Country-and-Western fan.

– He came to the house months back and I took care to have a good look, though the Aunts wouldn't let him see me – obviously didn't meet their exacting criteria.

– But what did he want? asked Jake, still all at sea.

– Well, as to what he *really* wanted, that's anyone's guess – but what he *said* was the usual thing.

– The usual thing?

– You know – my hand in marriage and all that.

– He – wanted to – *marry* you?

Jake felt the words were being dragged out of his throat on a length of chain.

– Of course – that's what they all want. As my Aunts

110

never tire of telling me, I am a young lady with prospects. It is my duty to make a suitable marriage, to preserve the family fortunes. Not throw myself away, like my mother did, she added in an undertone.

The irony of her tone eluded Jake, who was still grappling with the implications of what she had just said. He felt in his stomach that same spreading chill that comes when, in an exam you have completed with ease and confidence, you turn the paper ten minutes from the end and find a completely unnoticed set of questions on the back. That Helen should be routinely courted by grown men altered his perspective in an instant: a moment before it had seemed to him that it must be as clear to her as it was to him that they were made for each other, chosen from the very moment of their birth. Now he had a sudden vision of his true position in Helen's life – a stranger on the margin of a territory he knew little about and where counted for less. Of course she was not bothered about him and Alison! She had never even considered him in that light: he was just a boy she happened to know; that was all.

The only way to cope with the crushing humiliation was to turn away from it.

– What are we going to do? he said in a flat voice. We can't go to Silk House, but we can't *not* go either – not without giving away that we know what's happened there. I'm supposed to be away for at least a week, for god's sake! And what if my parents phone? Or if there's something about the murder on the television? O God!

Suddenly it was all just a big, *huge* mess: he buried his face in his hands, then, feeling he was being a bit theatrical, stared moodily out the window.

– I suppose we could go and say there was no-one there

111

when we arrived. That would be true, at least.

It sounded feeble, but it was the best he could think of.

– Unless the police were there, said Helen. Which is pretty likely. No, I don't think we can risk going near Silk House at all.

– We could just come back.

– And say what? said Helen, fiercely. That we changed our minds, for no reason? That'd be a dead giveaway!

– I suppose you're right.

– We have to go somewhere else entirely.

Her face took on an inward, thoughtful look.

– But wouldn't that be just the same? said Jake. We'd still have to come up with an explanation of why we changed our plans and didn't tell anyone.

– Come on, Jake – we're teenagers. We can say that we succumbed to temptation and went off together. They'll believe that. It's what people expect teenagers to do. You can say I led you astray. They'll believe that too, she added, with a small smile.

Jake looked at her, open-mouthed. The irony of her proposal was not lost on him. A few minutes ago, before the reality of where he stood with her had dawned on him, it would have been like the realization of his most secret fantasy to hear her say that, but now its seemed little more than a bitter joke – that they should make believe to do the very thing that she had just casually made clear was impossible in reality.

– So where do we run off to? he said heavily.

– London first, to my father's flat – we'll need somewhere to stay tonight. Then Paris.

– Paris?!

– Dad has an auction to go to there. We can catch the

112

Eurostar from Waterloo. My cousin Agnès should put us up.

Jake looked down, shaking his head in disbelief. What did you do in the holidays, then? O, I ran off with a girl – we spent the night in London, then went on to Paris. Paris in the Spring, you know – *the* romantic destination for teenage runaways. But it's all right, nothing happened really – we were just pretending.

He sat back and looked disconsolately out of the window: was ever a boy more cruelly mocked?

The rest of the journey passed, for Jake, in a grim daze. Helen slept: Jake wished he could, if only to shut out the complete futility of the situation he found himself in. What was he doing here? He didn't want to go traipsing along behind Helen on some wild goose chase. Sure, she wanted to find her father – but what made that his business? What made anything to do with her his business?

It was only once they were in London that his mood began to lift: the excitement of the city, with evening coming on and the lights shining brightly, the noise of the traffic and the bustle of the pavements, stirred his sluggish spirits. Just being there was adventure enough, no matter what else happened (or didn't happen, he reminded himself). Then outside Camden Town tube station something occurred that turned everything round again: Helen stopped suddenly.

– I can't do this, she said.

She was staring in front of her, watching something rerun before her eyes. Jake was startled to see that she was trembling. He put his arm round her.

– Come on, it's all right.

He felt her relax, leaning into him.

– I'm glad you're here, she said.

Her voice was scarcely more than a whisper. This was so unlike the bold and confident Helen that Jake was used to that he was seriously worried; but there was another part of him that could not help thinking this a favourable development.

– Just take it easy. It's all right.

He gave her a squeeze and began to walk her towards the flat. He tried to think of something else to say – "Remember the last time we were here?" seemed promising, but then he did remember – they had come in a taxi that time, full of high spirits, and had raced each other up the stairs because they were both starving – and the door to her father's flat was open, and he had that chill premonition that something was badly wrong... no, perhaps not such a good idea to recall that.

They were at the street door now. Helen's hand shook so much when she put it on the handle that Jake had to turn it for her.

– Hey now, he murmured. It's OK.

– This is really stupid, said Helen, trying to smile. I'm terrified!

– You're frightening me, now – I thought you didn't do 'scared?' Who's going to protect *me*?

That made her laugh. This is good, thought Jake. Things are going well. They went up the stairs. In front of her father's door, Helen glanced nervously at the fanlight as she fished for her key. The light was out.

– It's just that I've always thought of this as somewhere safe, she said, a bolt-hole I could run to. I don't think I'll ever see it that way again.

She turned the key in the lock, but didn't open the door.

– Do you want me to go in first?

Helen nodded gratefully. He pushed open the door, feeling very heroic. He reached a hand out to Helen.

– Come on in – it's all right, there's no one here.

She came in and closed the door and stood close up against him in the dark hall, her face almost touching his. Jake realised that he was holding his breath: he could feel his heart shaking his whole chest.

Then someone switched on the light.

13
Three's a Crowd

Helen and Jake stood paralysed, openmouthed, clutching each other. A tall, elegant woman with auburn hair cut in a bob was surveying them coolly from the other end of the hall.

– Now, you must be Helen, she said. And your friend is?

Her voice was pleasant, rather deep, with no identifiable accent.

– Who are you? demanded Helen, recovering her *sang froid*. And what are you doing in my father's flat?

– I might ask you the same thing. Does your father know you're in the habit of bringing boyfriends here in his absence?

Jake was astonished. It was the first time he had ever seen Helen non-plussed.

– But who are you? she repeated. My father's never mentioned you.

116

– Well, I can't think of any reason why he should, she said. Mention me to *you*, she added, emphasizing the last word.

– I suppose you're my father's mistress, said Helen primly.

The woman just smiled. She turned to Jake.

– I still don't know *your* name, she said, as if knowing Jake's name was the most important thing in the world to her.

– Jake.

– Mine's Zoë. (Helen curled her lip) Now that we've settled the formalities, perhaps you'd like to come in?

With that, she turned and headed back into the living room, leaving them no option but to follow. Jake looked at Helen. She frowned and stumped off down the hall, looking more like a petulant schoolgirl than he would ever have thought possible. The woman was standing by the fireplace, quite at ease, a glass of wine in her hand. She wore a simple, well-tailored black dress that showed her figure to advantage.

– May I offer you a glass of Frascati? (smiling sweetly at Helen) It's very light. No? Some juice, perhaps?

Helen glared; Jake shook his head. He might have been standing between two thunderclouds that were about to collide.

– Now, I'm sorry to be so old-fashioned, but I really could not countenance your sharing a room. It would be irresponsible of me.

Jake was captivated by the power-struggle he was witnessing: he had never seen Helen so comprehensively outmanoeuvred. He could see her reviewing her possible responses and finding none of them satisfactory: she looked as though she had something stuck in her throat.

– You weren't planning to stay here tonight? was the best she could manage.

– I think I have to, now, Zoë smiled back.

Jake shrugged. I think this is what's called an ironic situation, he mused. Here we are being prevented from doing something we hadn't planned to do anyway. He looked at Helen, his palms turned upwards, eyebrows cocked: what can we do? She gave him a look that would have cut metal, then exercised a woman's right to go to the bathroom in the middle of an argument she is losing, leaving Jake sitting on the sofa feeling very young indeed.

– Girls can be so headstrong at that age, said Zoë.

– I suppose so.

– But you, Jake, strike me as more the reflective type – am I right?

– Well I – I don't like to rush into things, if that's what you mean.

– That is just what I mean – you're circumspect.

– Am I? said Jake, startled, then added, well I suppose I am.

– You know it's natural that Helen should take against me at first.

She gave him a meaningful look, which Jake pondered, being circumspect.

– O, you mean her father, and all that.

She smiled at his comprehension.

– You're perceptive, too – I like that in a man.

This piece of outrageous flattery was delivered with precisely the right half-humorous tone which managed to suggest that she was kidding, but not entirely.

– I wonder, Jake, if you could be my friend?

She paused, and sipped her wine, looking at him over the rim of the glass, letting the strange playground-sounding request hang in the air.

    – I mean like a friend at court who speaks up for you – an advocate for my cause.

    – Your cause? asked Jake, not quite understanding.

    – Yes, I'm afraid that at the moment Helen has me nicely aligned for the wicked stepmother slot.

In fact Helen, at that moment, was thinking rather along those lines, as she contemplated the glass shelf in the bathroom where the insolent Zoë had arrayed her toiletries – you'd think she lived here, damn it, Helen thought, then considered that perhaps she did: it had never really occurred to her to think about that side of her father's life, and he had certainly never spoken of it to her. It was strange, she thought, that you could start off thinking you knew a person really well, then gradually discover you knew less and less about him. Her initial rage at Zoë had calmed: she looked at herself in the mirror, with her usual sensation of detachment – who is that person, looking out at me? Almost without thinking, she reached for the little scent bottle – Shalimar by Guerlain, she noted – and removed the stopper.

It was strange to register the look of shock that came over the face in the mirror and think, *that is me.* She half expected to see someone appear behind her, long cool fingers over her mouth and pressing the side of her neck –

There was no mistaking it: the scent was the same as she had smelt in Silk House, just before she passed out.

In the sitting room, Jake was beginning to enjoy his conversation with Zoë: she had a way of talking to him, an easy familiarity, that put him at ease – he might have known her for ages. Then Helen came back and the temperature plummeted by about twenty degrees.

– Let's get something to eat, she said tersely. Leave your bag – we can fight over who sleeps on the sofa when we come back.

Jake rose rather wearily: he would have much preferred to stay and eat with Zoë, but a glance at Helen's face told him the idea was a non-starter. He gave Zoë an apologetic look, as if to say "what can a man do?" She cocked an amused eyebrow.

– Don't feel you have to stay in for our sake, said Helen. I have my own key.

Zoë smiled: Helen slammed the door. In the hall, Jake was surprised to see that Helen had her bag on her shoulder, and her finger to her lips, enjoining silence.

– Come on, she said, pulling him by the arm.

Outside on the pavement, a bemused Jake found himself shepherded past the Turkish restaurant, with its mouthwatering smells; Helen lunged out onto the roadway to hail a passing black cab.

– Where are we going?

– Waterloo – come on, get in!

– Waterloo? Isn't there anywhere nearer we can eat?

– To catch a train, stupid. We have to get out of here!

– What's the rush?

She told him about the perfume: he received it sceptically, saying that there might conceivably be more than one woman in London who wore Guerlain perfume – a suggestion which he supplemented, rather rashly, with the observation that he believed his mother used the same stuff.

– What train are we getting anyway? he asked, after

some minutes of frosty silence.

    – The Eurostar to Paris.

    – What?! But what about my bag?

    – Fortunes of war – we had to leave it, to make her think we'd come back.

    – I notice you brought yours.

    – Well, mine has important stuff in it.

Unlike mine, of course, thought Jake.

    – Like what? Your clean underwear?

    – Like your passport, if you must know.

    – My passport?

    – I filched it from your bedroom, she said coolly, enjoying his consternation. Well, you didn't know you were going to Paris, did you?

    – You really are something else, you know that?

The rest of the journey passed in unamiable silence.

14
The City of Light

Under chestnut trees in Paris in a café on the Boulevard Saint-Michel they made a kind of truce. Their arrival late the night before on the doorstep of Helen's cousin Agnès had been greeted with no more enthusiasm than could be expected: Helen had to be at her inventive best to produce a plausible reason for their being there, one that drew heavily on her father's reputation for fecklessness – he had been supposed to meet them but there had been some muddle over the trains, and now they hoped to catch him at the auction house next day, so could they please stay the night?

Now after a morning recovering Jake's wardrobe at Helen's expense they sat warily sipping coffee in warm spring sunshine.

– All right, said Jake, but what if he's not at either of the auction houses?

Helen winced. She felt for a moment like hitting Jake,

which was hardly fair, since it was a perfectly reasonable question; it just happened to be one she had been particularly trying to avoid thinking about. Her father *had* to be at *one* of the auction houses, because if he was not, where could he be? And of course the answer to that was that he could be anywhere, but Helen's growing fear ever since she had seen that horrible man, crouched and predatory on the stair outside his flat, was that he might be nowhere.

– What's the matter? asked Jake eventually, struck by her lack of response.

Helen hesitated on the verge of saying everything.

– Um – nothing, she said.

– Fine, said Jake heavily. Don't tell me then.

He looked around him in irritation. All about them, the City of Light bustled with life. Horns blared as traffic piled up behind a small van delivering vegetables; determined-looking students hurried to their classes, while less determined ones meandered down the boulevard; ancient gentlemen beamed at young mothers and their tottering infants, enjoying the spring sunshine. There were couples just like them at every other table, but unlike them, they all seemed to be having a good time and enjoying one another's company.

– Come on, he said. How far is it to the first auction house anyway?

– You don't have to come if you don't want to.

– I've said I'd come, so I will, rejoined Jake.

He was aware as he said it that he didn't really want to go, but equally he didn't want to give Helen licence to let him off: if she hadn't wanted him to come, she shouldn't have asked him in the first place. He stalked after her, glowering.

They drew a blank at the first place near the *Musée*

d'Orsay, which was very slick and modern, all soft lighting and fish-tanks, with people in expensive suits murmuring discreetly about the lots, none of which looked more than a couple of years old. Helen embarrassed him by talking in a loud voice about what rubbish it all was, safe art for corporate buyers, not her father's kind of thing at all – it was Jake's impression that she did it on purpose to annoy him. In reality, she was doing it to distract herself from the fact that there was probably only one more opportunity to find her father before the trail went cold: Mamoulian Frères in the 9th Arrondissement.

Mamoulian Frères was very much Helen's father's sort of place: its marvellously over-the-top baroque interior, all gilt plaster curlicues, housed an equally baroque clientele, drawn from the four corners of the earth – some looked to have breezed in from Moroccan *souks* or the immemorial markets on the Silk Road, or Samarkhand. Here was a Russian émigré, complete with astrakhan collar, gold pince-nez and goatee beard; here beringed Arabs in full dress conversed in hushed tones; there a pair of identical twins in short silk dresses – one green, one blue – looked like something from the nineteen-twenties, with their long cigarette holders, head scarves and strings of pearls.

Gerald De Havilland stood in the midst of it all, absorbing the atmosphere: he loved auctions, especially at this end of the market, where the possibility of acquiring some obscure piece that turned out be really valuable was balanced about evenly with the chance of being landed with something completely spurious. Around him, the major lots were displayed in glass cases perched on ornate stands – although, as a security measure, the smaller articles displayed were often duplicates, ever since a daring raid in the nineties when thieves had set off smoke bombs and managed to clear out a cool few millions' worth of easily portable treasures. That was the case with his own object of interest – the crystal displayed as the Stone of Sorrow was, he knew, a cut-glass copy: the real one was in the auctioneer's safe.

The auction had been in progress for about forty minutes, and De Havilland had been careful to pursue a number of other lots – partly, he admitted, for the thrill of it, but chiefly to disguise his real intentions – his aim was to appear a languid, dilettante buyer, whiling away an afternoon with no particular object in mind, content to go home empty-handed if his *ennui* was alleviated just a little. He wondered how many of his fellow-bidders were engaged in the same pretence – at least half, he reckoned. One certainly was not: a tall man in a linen suit, sporting a flamboyant peacock-blue waistcoat, seemed so drawn by the Stone that he could scarcely keep his eyes off it; indeed, having been drawn into the orbit of the display case, he seemed unable to leave it – every now and then he would sidle away from it a few steps, only to jerk to a halt on the end of an invisible tether; then he would look round, rolled catalogue held to his lips, trying to discern who might be his rival bidders.

De Havilland had spotted at least one – a tall woman in black with a big white hat that hid her face in shadow seemed to be watching the behaviour of waistcoat man with quiet amusement; she was about the same distance on the other side of the display case as De Havilland was on this, and so far she had not taken part in any bidding. Catching her eye, he gave her an amiable smile.

At a word from the auctioneer, the attendant – gorgeously clad in the red and gold livery of an eighteenth-century footman, complete with white silken hose, matching gloves and powdered wig – made his way towards the case containing the duplicate Stone, to indicate that it was the next lot up. De Havilland, outwardly calm and insouciant as ever, felt an involuntary tightening of his throat. His fingers tensed their grip on his bidding paddle.

The bidding proceeded in a desultory manner, with brief shows of interest scattered throughout the crowd, but no real enthusiasm betrayed as yet: to De Havilland's surprise, the man in the waistcoat made no attempt to take part. He wondered at that, then guessed that perhaps he was hoping to do some sort of post-auction deal – if he stayed out of the bidding just now, and there was no great show of interest, the lot would go for a low price, allowing him to make a generous offer afterwards to whoever bought it – it was often a surer way to secure an item you really wanted than to bid openly for it, which generally forced up the price as well. He had considered doing the same himself, but now he reckoned he would rather secure it in the auction room, so that if the waistcoat man wanted to buy, he would be the seller.

The auctioneer was showing signs of impatience at the slowness of the bidding, and made some effort to talk up the lot, referring to its curious history and mysterious origins – experts were unable to say even what it was made of, but it was attested to be harder than diamond. De Havilland smiled, sensing that he had misjudged his audience: it was just as he had hoped – the Stone appeared no more than an oddball item, much too large and heavy for an item of jewellery, and with little prospect of being cut into smaller stones. After a decent pause, he entered a bid with a languid flap of his paddle, seeming barely able to work up enough energy to raise it; in the silence that followed, he strove to appear as uninterested as possible in the outcome, turning to remark to his neighbour that it really was all rather too dull this afternoon.

No counter bid.

The auctioneer darted his eyes about the room, calculated swiftly that he was flogging a dead horse, and brought down his gavel.

Going once.

De Havilland yawned extravagantly and looked about him, disappointed that there was to be no competition.

Going...

He observed the waistcoat man manoeuvring to get closer to him: he could not see the woman in the white hat – no, there she was, looking on with the same expression of amusement – she too had entered no bid: was she playing the same game as the waistcoat man, looking for a private deal?

Gone!

The gavel came down with a crack: De Havilland pursed his lips and rolled his eyes, like one who has made a joke and finds it has been taken seriously. The man in the waistcoat was heading in his direction.

Jake and Helen had arrived in the gallery not long before the final bid: Helen hung over the rail, scanning the crowd eagerly; Jake looked too, with a more jaundiced eye.

– There he is! said Helen, then raised her hand to her mouth in mock consternation. O, no!

– What is it? asked Jake, still trying to pick him out.

– That man he's with – in the light coloured suit – it's my gentleman caller!

– Great, muttered Jake between gritted teeth.

Does she have to sound so excited about it? he thought bitterly, not realizing that Helen's delight was simply at seeing her father. He gazed morosely at the crowd, and managed to find Gerald De Havilland at last, talking to a tall man whose back was to the gallery.

– You go down, he said. I'll wait up here.

Helen gave him an odd look: her own face was beaming.

– You don't want to lose him in the crowd, said Jake.

– O, right! said Helen, and hurried off down the stairs.

By the time she emerged into the hall, the crowd had thinned where her father was, and she spotted him right away; turning to the gallery, she gave Jake the thumbs up, then hurried to meet him.

– Helen!

– Hi Dad.

She turned to the man in the linen suit.

– Hello, Mr. Raeburn – come to ask my father for my hand, have you?

– Your *father*? said Raeburn, with a startled look.

– Of course, said Helen, extending her hand for him to kiss.

Raeburn – either entering into the spirit of things, or else to cover his evident confusion, bowed low over it, his lips brushing her fingers.

– Do you two know one another? asked her father, astonished.

– We have met, said Helen.

– But what on earth are you doing here?

– I came with Jake.

She glanced up at the balcony, to signal him to come down, but he was no longer there.

15
Crystal History

Jake had stayed in the gallery just long enough to witness the encounter between Helen and the man in the linen suit – whose face he still could not see – before turning away in disgust and stomping down the stairs. One part of him at least was aware that he was using what he had seen as an excuse to vent his ill-temper, but it felt good all the same – and somehow the very anonymity of his rival helped stoke his resentment. He was not going to be dragged all this way so that, at the drop of a hat, Helen could abandon him for some faceless stranger; he would go straight back to the flat, collect his passport, and head for home –

As he emerged into the foyer, he was aware of someone falling into step beside him: turning, he saw a tall woman, elegantly dressed in black, with a large white hat angled so she could not fully see her face. Then she turned towards him.

– Hello Jake – are you going in my direction?

It was Zoë.

*

Helen and her father sat in the café adjoining the auction house: on the other side of the table was Macintosh Raeburn, clearly in a state of some excitement, yet puzzled at something too.

– So, Mr. De Havilland, you will have guessed why I am here?

– You are interested in the Stone of Sorrow?

– Interested? said Raeburn, with a complicated look, part scorn, part anguish. Yes, I suppose you could say that…though *fascinated* would perhaps be a better word – some (my ex-wife, for instance!) might even say *infatuated*. Yes, I have been interested in your Stone of Sorrow for most of my life – though that is not the name I would give it.

– Indeed? queried De Havilland, with eyebrows raised.

– Do you know anything of its history? said Raeburn, almost fiercely.

– A little, said De Havilland blandly. I was planning to do some research –

– Perhaps I could save you the trouble, interrupted Raeburn.

– Well, I don't know if I'd want you to, De Havilland smiled. I find that's half the fun, with such curiosities – trying to discover where they came from.

Helen looked at Raeburn, who struck her as a perfect illustration of a man in two minds about something – one part of him was evidently in the grip of some strong emotion, a passion he mastered only with difficulty – but the other part was distracted by something else entirely, something that he couldn't quite work out, but which seemed to centre on Helen's father, from the way he kept looking at him, then glancing away again.

– But in the end, your researches would only lead you to me, he said. There is no one else can tell you about it.

His voice was an odd mixture of anger and pleading. De Havilland eyed him coolly.

– Very well – I'm in no rush to go anywhere.

Raeburn, now that he had the opportunity, seemed uncertain where to start – he started to speak several times, then shook his head in irritation. Eventually Helen's father said, not unkindly,

– Why not take the Red King's advice, Mr. Raeburn? Begin at the beginning, and go right through until you come to the end.

– Eh? What? Well I suppose that might just do – but there is one scene that keeps intruding itself, so I'd better get that out of the way first – it comes much later in the story, but I'll ask you to hold it in mind while I tell you the rest.

Helen smiled at her father as Raeburn leaned forward, elbows on the table, hands held out towards them, as in offering – his eyes gleamed with excitement.

– You are in the court of the Duke of Milan: it is the beginning of the 16th century. The court is in mourning: it is less than a week since a young noblewoman – perhaps the Duke's niece, just possibly his daughter – has been laid to rest in the family vaults after dying in mysterious circumstances. Dark rumours abound – it is said that the Duke himself ordered her death, after a mission she was engaged on failed. However it is, the Duke is in sombre mood, and has ordered all but a few attendants away as he discusses affairs of state with his cousin, the Cardinal Archbishop of Milan.

All at once there is a commotion in the corridor – not the one leading to the private apartments, but on the other side, leading to the vaults. Then, before the horrified eyes of the half-dozen people there, a grotesque figure lurches into the room – as one of the witnesses said, "it walked like a puppet, in a jerky manner, throwing out its arms and legs". Another remarked that "it seemed bound together by flickering ropes of green light". All attested that it was the corpse of the girl they had recently entombed, reanimated by some sorcery, for it was undoubtedly dead, as the state of the body made clear – it was high summer, and the weather had been very hot.

Helen felt her gorge rise.

– What happened? she asked, with difficulty.

– The corpse attempted a murderous attack on the Duke – it had a knife – but the demand on the disintegrating body proved too great, and it burst into flames.

– Yeeugh! said Helen. Her father looked sceptical.

– All this is set down in great detail in a file in the Vatican Library, said Raeburn, though you need special permission to see it – fortunately I know a Cardinal or two. But as I said, all that happens much later on in the story – we'll come back to it.

– I can hardly wait, said Helen, pulling a face.

Raeburn sat back in his chair, eyed them both to see that he had their full attention, then continued his tale.

– As for where the story starts, you have to go a long way back for that – some twenty-seven centuries – and even then it's not the real beginning, because they found it there when they arrived – Byzas of Megara and his party of merchant adventurers, sailing North towards the Black Sea to found a colony, on the advice of the Oracle at Delphi – "in the country opposite the land of the blind" it told him, and when he saw the wonderful natural harbour that the Chalcedonians on the opposite shore had somehow managed to miss, he reckoned that must be the place.

The site they chose was on a headland, and there was a curious rock-formation there, like some sort of stack or standing-stone, and in the middle of their celebrations – founding a city called for all manner of religious ritual, sacrifices to the gods, libations poured out on the ground and so on – this stack was struck by a bolt of lightning, out of a clear blue sky, or so the story goes; and after they'd picked themselves up from the shock, they saw that the rock had disintegrated, to reveal something that must have been inside it – a sort of statue, on a pillar.

– A statue? said Helen.

– They called it the Bronze Basilisk, though it certainly wasn't bronze, since it didn't tarnish, and probably wasn't what we'd call a basilisk either, which is a sort of little crowned serpent – this thing, by all accounts, had a serpent's tail, "naked pinions" – which I take to mean featherless wings, like a bat's – but a bird's head, with a beak like an eagle, and wearing a sort of crown. There was a lever on its back. When it was drawn back, a small hatch or portal opened to reveal the Basilisk's heart.

– Its heart? asked Helen.

– I'll tell you about that in a moment. When the lever was thrown forward, a beam of light shone from the Basilisk's beak, and wonders were revealed.

He paused dramatically, glaring round the table.

– Wonders were revealed? echoed Helen, slowly.

– Or miracles were shown: the Greek name can mean either: *Thaumatophane*.

– What sort of wonders?

– Apparently, they defied description. As you can imagine, they reckoned it was something fairly special and sacred, being revealed to them like that right at the founding of their city, so they built a special shrine for it, and established a religious cult. The city they founded was Byzantium – which became Constantinople, and is now Istanbul

– Its heart, said Helen, you forgot to say about that.

Raeburn gave them a long look, weighing some ponderous utterance.

– Its heart was a glowing crystal.

Helen's father pursed his lips and put his head on one side.

– And you think that crystal is, well, *this* crystal?

– I know it!

– What makes you so certain? asked De Havilland, eyeing him sceptically. Don't tell me – because it *has* to be?

Raeburn looked a bit flustered, as if the words had been taken out of his mouth. After some spluttering, he said

– It is not entirely clear why the Thaumatophane fell into disuse, but it did. Some say it simply broke – others suggest darker, more complex reasons, hinting that the operation of the machine – what it showed or revealed – was somehow influenced by the will or character of the operator, so that if the operator was corrupt, then so too were the visions – there is also a reference which says "the people were no longer content to watch the visions, but began to take part in them" – it's not clear what that meant, but soon afterwards the cult was either suppressed or, more probably, restricted to an elite group, the so-called Guardians of the Crystal – what seems certain is that the crystal was now kept separately.

At some point – again it's not clear why – the internal

mechanism was dismantled and removed, and the Bronze Basilisk was reduced to a mere shell – it's my guess that the iconoclasts destroyed it in the eighth century. But the crystal survived – Michael Scot knew about it in the thirteenth century and was actively seeking it at the time of his death –

– Michael Scot? said Helen. The same one that's in Dante's *Inferno*?

– Could well be – he was a famous mediaeval wizard: he came from Scotland – Balwearie, in Fife, probably – studied mathematics here in Paris – and magic too, some said – and ended up as Court Astrologer to the Emperor Frederick, in Sicily – he was reputed to be the greatest adept of the Middle Ages. He was a scholar of Arabic, which is probably how he learned about the *Thaumatophane* – it was from the Islamic world that Europe recovered all the classical learning that had been lost in the Dark Ages, and a lot more besides – did you know that there were more than a hundred book shops in tenth-century Baghdad? That was at a time when few people in Europe could even read!

– Not something we're very ready to admit, said Helen's father, that Western civilization was founded on Islamic scholarship.

– Indeed not, said Raeburn, but it's true all the same. Anyway, Scot sought the crystal, and the dispersed parts of the Thaumatophane, but he didn't complete the task, because the same quest was taken up three centuries later, by the Mage Albanus – who was, like Scot, reckoned the greatest adept of his age. He was for some time in the service of the Duke of Milan – which brings us back to where I started.

One of the things that Albanus did for the Duke was provide him with emissaries – spies, in truth – but of a rather special sort. Do you know the word *metempsychosis*?

– The transmigration of souls, said Helen. Plato talks about it in the *Republic*. It's like reincarnation – after death, your soul migrates to someone else, and is reborn, so that all your knowledge is actually recollected from your past life – *anamnesis*, he called it.

– Well, well! said Raeburn. I am impressed! But Albanus's *metempsychosis* was of a rather different sort – perhaps it would be more accurate to call it *soul-projection*. It appears that he could put himself into a deep trance – from which his servants were expressly forbidden to wake him, lest it prove fatal – and project the greater part of his vital force into someone else's body and so take control of it –

– You mean a *dead* body? said Helen.

– Not generally, no – but we'll come to that in a moment. No, the whole point was to control the body *through* its living owner – "so the coachman goes but where his master directs him," as the Vatican Archive quaintly puts it – a bit like taking a taxi, I suppose.

At this point, Helen's father leaned forward, a look of intense interest on his face.

– You can see the advantage, of course, said Raeburn. You have a messenger you can send to the court of your enemies who is effectively – well, a bugging device, you would have to say, but more than that too – you can hear with his ears and see with his eyes, and you can give him instructions on the spot, tell him what to say and do –

Helen noticed with alarm that her father's face had gone white: he didn't look at all well. Raeburn, wrapped up in his tale, went on.

– When Albanus left his service, the Duke was immediately afraid he would use the same powers against him, in the service of his rivals, so he arranged an assassination attempt. He sent a woman – Albanus was said to be susceptible in that department – in the hope that she could get close enough to him to kill him; but Albanus discovered the plan and took possession of the woman, and sent her back against the Duke – who, being a suspicious sort, had her ambushed and killed – though as you've already heard, that still wasn't quite enough to thwart Albanus.

– He reanimated a corpse? said Helen's father, in scarcely more than a whisper.

– Well, according to the learned Dominicans who conducted the Vatican inquiry, the corpse was never entirely *de*animated, since although the young woman's soul was deemed to have fled when she was strangled, sufficient of Albanus's vital force remained within her body to maintain its function – though very imperfectly, as the descriptions make clear, and only by a prodigious expenditure of energy.

Helen, looking at her father, was concerned that he was going to pass out – she wanted to stop Raeburn and help him, yet at the same time she wanted to hear the end of the story.

– But what does all this have to do with the crystal? she urged desperately, hoping that perhaps a switch of subject might ease her father's distress.

– I was coming to that. The Duke had Albanus exiled on pain of death, as a sorcerer, and he had to go to France, which did not suit him at all, as he was involved in some project which required the kind of workmanship that could only be found in Italy at that time – so he engaged an agent to act on his behalf, but the agent betrayed him – Albanus was lured to Ferrara on the promise of a safe conduct from the Duke there, but he turned out to be married to the Duke of Milan's sister, and he had Albanus seized and burned at the stake. For his reward, the traitor "asked something of the Duke that had been the wizard's, and this the Duke gladly gave". That something was the thaumatophanic crystal.

– How do you know? asked Helen.

– Because it appears in the only portrait of the traitorous agent that is known to exist, one that was painted not long after Albanus was betrayed – a painting that I know is familiar to you, since it is part of your family collection –

He smiled at the dawning comprehension on Helen's face.

– Yes, it is the same one that was found in the boot of a Mercedes registered to Aurelian Pounce, parked beside that house in Forcalquier that was so mysteriously wrecked last summer – *The Secret of the Alchemist*, I believe it is called.

– Ruggiero da Montefeltro betrayed Albanus? breathed Helen.

Raeburn nodded, smiling.

– In exchange for the crystal which your father has apparently just bought – though that is something I can't quite work out – but I rather think I had best be going now: all this seems to have proved a little too much for Mr. De Havilland. Here's my card – I expect you'll want to get in touch.

He rose and, still smiling, left the room.

16
Elgin Marbles

Jake needed little persuasion to accompany Zoë to a café across the road, all carved wood and old mirrors showing *fin-de-siècle* gentlemen in luxuriant moustaches and bowler hats being served absinthe by goddess-like *art nouveau* women. They took a table in a little wooden booth. Zoë gave him a slow smile from underneath her hat.

– Well now, isn't this a surprise?

Her tone suggested it was anything but.

– It is for me, Jake rejoined.

Another smile.

– I was hoping you might do me a favour.

– Ye-e-es? queried Jake.

– I rather hoped you might introduce me to Gerald De Havilland.

– But – I thought – aren't you – ?

– Well, evidently not, since I've never met him, she smiled.

– But back in London – didn't you – ?

– I fell in with Helen's suggestion – it's a useful trick, if you ever need to assume an identity – just take the one that people give you.

Smiling mysteriously, she removed her hat, and set it on the bench beside her.

– Who you are is so much a matter of context – in London, at ease in his flat, I was Gerald De Havilland's mistress. But now, here in Paris – *voilà*! I am someone quite different.

With a flourish, she detached her copper-coloured hair and laid it on the table, where it lay between them like some exotic sea-creature washed up on a beach. Her own hair was dark, close cropped. Like an actress, thought Jake. Without the wig she looked younger, almost boyish.

– But – if you're not, well, you know – then what were you doing in his flat?

– Investigating.

– Are you – from the police? Jake asked, suddenly fearful, his mind making lightning connections between Silk House and Helen's father's flat.

– Not the police.

– So you're just a burglar then? he said, lighthearted with relief.

– I can be, if the need arises. All part of the job, she added, with another smile.

– And just what is your job?

– You could say that I work undercover.

– You mean like the secret service?

She laughed.

– Well *like* them, but not quite so glamorous – I'm with Culture & Heritage.

Jake managed to turn his incredulous laugh into a

snorting sort of cough.

– Culture and Heritage? Isn't that old castles, and museums and stuff?

– And what's so funny about that? she said with mock indignation. Never heard of the Elgin Marbles?

Jake considered: he knew that Elgin was a town somewhere near Inverness, and marbles of course was a game you played in primary school – bools was its proper name in Scotland. Somehow he did not think Zoë meant that. He shook his head.

– Lord Elgin was the British Ambassador to Greece, in the days when it was under Turkish control. He bought a great quantity of classical antiquities – marble statues, friezes and so on – and shipped them back to Britain, where they are still on display in the British Museum. Ever since Greece regained her independence, she has been demanding their return. It's a big political issue.

Jake was all at sea.

– Er, I'm not quite sure I follow you.

– I just wanted to make the point that some countries – most of them now, that have any – guard their Culture and Heritage jealously. You must have noticed the fuss when someone abroad buys an old painting or piece of sculpture and wants to take it out of the country – most countries now require a licence to export ancient artefacts, and it's not very often granted.

She watched him, smiling slightly. Wheels began to turn in Jake's mind. *Ancient artefacts*. So that was what all this was about! At the back of his mind he had always wondered a little about the legality of Stephen Langton's just taking the Alchemist's Machine – finders keepers was all very well in the playground, but not in the real world. He felt he had stopped on the very edge of a precipice: if he said the wrong thing now, he could get all sorts of people into trouble – including himself.

Zoë watched him waver anxiously for a time, then decided to rescue him.

– It's all right, Jake – as I said, I'm not the police. Recovery is what we're interested in, not prosecution. In fact there's generally a reward of some sort – though of course we can't compete with wealthy unscrupulous collectors, she frowned. If they really want a piece, some people are prepared to pay – and do – just about anything.

She shot him a meaningful look. *Just about anything – like having another collector murdered*, thought Jake. He was in a real quandary now: he wanted to help Zoë, but what could he tell her? *You're too late – Mr. Langton's been murdered and the machine's been stolen?* Explaining that would lead him to places he would rather not go. On the other hand, could he really just introduce her to Helen's father – what if she was from the police?

– Why do you want me to introduce you? Why not just go up to him yourself?

– A shrewd question, Jake. I need to meet him on friendly terms, to gain his confidence. If I approached him cold, he'd just shut me out.

Sounds reasonable, thought Jake. They're probably still across in the auction rooms. I could take her there now – but there was something he wanted to know first. Watching her closely, he said

– You were at Silk House, weren't you?

She put her head to one side, raising her eyebrows and sticking out her lower lip, acknowledging that he had made a shrewd hit.

- Did Helen tell you that?
- She recognized your perfume.
- Sharp girl! You'll need to watch her, Jake – you'll not be able to carry on behind *her* back!

Jake smiled at the flattery, but he was smart enough to notice that she was leading him away from something. He led her right back.

- So did you kill Stephen Langton?

If his bluntness surprised her, she didn't show it – she just gave him the same, half-humorous, weighing-him-up sort of look.

- Well, I suppose I could have, she said. What is it they consider? Means, motive and opportunity? Well, I certainly had the opportunity, or I would have if I'd been there a bit earlier...and I'm sure I could have found the means...you might reckon from what I've just told you that I had the motive, too – but then, why would I still be here? If the Alchemist's Machine is what I'm after – and you're quite right, she said, catching the glint in his eye, that *is* what this is all about – then I would hardly do anything as drastic as killing someone unless it was the only sure way to get hold of it, would I? And if I'd already got it, as I say, why would I still be here, trying to persuade you to introduce me to Gerald De Havilland?

Jake sat awhile, considering this – it struck him as a pretty fair point, and her candour was disarming: she made no attempt to deny that she was there, or even that she was a reasonable suspect for the murder – would she be as cool as that if she *had* done it? He still hesitated about introducing her to Helen's father, but on the other hand he was tempted by the prospect of turning up with a beautiful woman, especially if Helen was still entertaining her "gentleman caller" – that would show *her*!

– When do you want to meet him? I think they're probably still across the road.

– O, I'm not in any particular hurry, she said, to Jake's surprise. It was just the arrangement I wanted to be sure of – as a matter of fact, I would rather delay it just a bit – will you be around tomorrow?

Well, I hadn't planned to be, thought Jake, but that was before I met you. He nodded his assent.

– Good! Now, you'll have to excuse me a moment. I have a phone call to make.

She produced a dainty mobile phone from her bag, pressed a couple of buttons and waited, the phone pressed against her ear; in the meantime she gave Jake a smile of complicity, as though he was an important part of what she was phoning about. Then someone must have answered; she began to speak rapidly in a language Jake did not recognize – it sounded a bit like Italian, but he knew enough Italian to know it wasn't that. When the conversation was done, she gave Jake another smile, apologetic this time.

– It's an international business, this.

– Er, what government did you say you represented? ventured Jake

– I didn't, she said with a disarming smile.

– And you're not going to?

– Let's just say I represent the rightful owners.

Another smile, signalling the matter was closed. She gathered up her wig and stuffed it in her handbag, then picked up her hat.

– And now, I fear I must tear myself away.

– But – how do I get in touch with you?

– Don't worry, I'll find you, she smiled.

He tried a last parting shot.

– But if you didn't kill him – who did?

She gave an enigmatic smile, and turned her hands out, pleading ignorance, but the expression on her face contradicted the shrug.

– Who do *you* think? she asked.

And she turned on her heel and was gone, leaving a faint whiff of perfume, while Jake was still collecting his thoughts.

17
Revelations

– There's something I have to tell you, Helen.

Helen faced her father across the room. He looked more normal now, only very tired. All at once she felt that now, before he spoke, was the time to tell him.

– Before you say anything, Dad, there's something *I* have to tell *you*.

Her words pulled him up short. She could see him begin to rehearse the list of things that might prompt a teenage girl to say that to her father. Quickly, before he went off on completely the wrong track, she said

– Stephen Langton is dead. He was murdered.

– What? No!

She was relieved to see how shocked he was: he clearly had no idea. He buried his head in his hands.

– God, that is my fault, he said between his fingers.

He sat for a time, working this out. Then he looked at her, and said,

    – But it rather alters what I have to say to you.

He took a deep breath, and looked at her steadily.

    – I think I killed a man.

He saw the sudden doubt flit across her face, and went on quickly.

    – No, it wasn't Stephen…in fact, I think it was the man who killed him.

    – What – what happened? asked Helen, barely above a whisper.

    – I was on my way to Waterloo Station and he jumped me. There's a very lonely bit there, just after you cross Westminster Bridge, where it's all intersections under bridges, very deserted and poorly lit. I thought I was being followed, but I couldn't see anyone, then he came out of the shadows just ahead of me – don't ask me how he got there. I thought I'd be a match for him – he was quite a small man – but he was frighteningly strong, and he had a knife. It was all I could do to keep him from sticking it in my throat – then something strange happened: he suddenly seemed to lose all sense of what he was doing: you know, like he had just woken up – and he just stopped trying to stab me; and I was still resisting with all my strength, so the knife went back into his throat…her father stared ahead of him, seeming to see it all happening again. He just hung there, on the knife, then gave a sort of gurgle, and slid off the blade, down among some dustbins… I left him there, and doubled back to the bridge and threw the knife in the river. There was no-one about – I needed to catch the train, so I forced myself to go back, though I kept to the other side of the road… I'm pretty sure I must have killed him.

– O, Dad! breathed Helen.

She stared at him for a time in shocked silence, aware that the thought uppermost in her mind was not that her father had killed a man, but whether he was likely to get caught. From the sound of it, no one had seen him, and the knife was at the bottom of the Thames…she wondered how much of a stir it would cause: she supposed that London had its share of violent deaths, like any great city.

– Who was he? she asked after a time.

– A Romanian – he called himself Dr. Sarden Negulescu.

– What – what makes you think he killed Stephen?

– Well, he said after a long pause, that's what I have to tell you about…

And he unfolded the whole story from the beginning, with the little doctor's mistaking him for Stephen Langton, and his guess that it would be wise to clear out to London – "I had a pretty shrewd idea that he would come back to try and steal the machine, but it never struck me that he would find Stephen there when he did, but that's what must have happened…I suppose I just assumed he'd be away longer: he was never one to leave a note of his whereabouts." When it came to the account of selling the machine, Helen realised with a shock how close her father had been when she had her terrifying encounter on the stair – what might she have done, had she known? Still, there was no point in thinking about that now; and at least there was one good thing, and that was that the cursed Machine was out of their lives now – when she said so, her father gave her an odd, considering look; then at length he said

– Well, I hope it's done with, anyway.

– You mean you think it isn't? asked Helen with a sudden chill of fear.

– It was when Raeburn started talking about soul-projection and taking over other people to use them as messengers – I'm pretty sure that's what was happening with Negulescu.

– What!?

– You see, it's happened to me before – when Aurelian Pounce was after me for the painting…only it can't be Pounce this time.

Helen looked around her, surprised to find the room still bright: she felt the shadows were closing in on her.

– Who do you think it is? she said.

– I don't know – but I wonder if there is someone who might be able to tell us?

He picked up Raeburn's card from the table.

– There's something I'd like you to do for me.

***

When Helen arrived at the flat, she half expected a fight, but Jake was in such a conciliatory mood that she immediately wondered if he was up to something.

– I was speaking to your cousin – she says there's a really good exhibition on at the Pompidou centre: fancy going to it tomorrow?

– Yes – sure, said Helen, a little surprised. Let's do that.

– So – what time then? said Jake, yawning. Nine o'clock? Ten?

Helen hesitated, thinking.

– Mmm – let's make it a bit later. Eleven, maybe? It's just that I've something to attend to first.

– O? said Jake, with a questioning look.

– It's nothing, said Helen. Just family business.

149

They held one another's gaze for a long moment, each trying to fathom what the other was holding back. Helen broke the tension with a smile.

– I'm worn out, she said. I'll see you in the morning.

She headed for her bedroom; Jake stood looking after her, a thoughtful expression on his face.

18

Stupor Mundi

Helen was sure she would go straight to sleep as soon as she reached her bed, if indeed she got that far – it was almost too much effort to pull off her clothes and struggle into her nightdress; but no sooner had she done so than she felt wakeful and alert, and curiously purposeful. It seemed there was something she just *had* to do – but what? She was not perhaps as surprised as she should have been when the answer popped into her head: *Sophie's book*. She had not thought about it since the night she had found it in Switzerland – did not even recall if she had packed it – yet standing here now in her cousin's Paris bedroom (how warm the night was! She really must open a window) she felt certain that she would find she had.

Sure enough, there it was in the outside pocket of her bag, as pleasing to look at as ever (and to handle – she felt a distinct tingle as she picked it up) – how odd that she could have so completely forgotten it until now. She settled herself on the bed, her pillows propped up behind her, and opened it at random.

The peculiar thing was that when she was about to open it, she had not the least recollection of what she had read before, but as soon as she touched the page (and there was that odd *frisson* again – a slight but perceptible shock) it was all present to her mind, as though it had been there all the time, like a scene on stage waiting for the curtain to be raised. In the same way, she recalled without surprise how the book worked, and instead of looking at the page she had opened, she touched it with her fingers.

Vividly into her mind there came a smell, or rather a feeling, a sense of atmosphere, that was as intense and immediate as a smell – there was heat in it, and pungency, and the tang of the sea – yet mingled with it was a coolness, a clarity like pure water drawn from a deep well. This was a paradoxical place, where the heat of passion coexisted with cool clear thought, where human warmth and vigour was allied to calculating mind, detached and objective to the point of cruelty. There was a sense also of intermingling, of cross currents – to the North, something awakening from long slumber, hungry for knowledge; in a crescent Southward, from East to West, something in its prime, at the high noon of its culture and learning; but North-Eastward something much more ancient, a wisdom stretching back to the roots of time. Here they met and flowed together – but where was *here*?

In answer came a sound like a sea whisper: *Sicily*.

The spicy, pungent, many-layered atmosphere seemed to transform into a whirlpool of colours, orange red yellow brown blue green, from which emerged at length a face – a striking face, forceful rather than handsome, crowned with fiery hair, broad browed, with a long straight nose, determined mouth and wide-set intelligent eyes – eyes with a look of most striking boldness: a man used to command, who has never in his life had to defer to anyone. I was wrong, thought Helen, the currents do not just flow here, they are drawn by this man, as by a vortex – for this is surely *Stupor Mundi* himself, the Wonder of the World, the Holy Roman Emperor Frederick II, scholar-warrior-architect-poet, fluent in six languages and celebrated throughout the world for the breadth and depth of his learning. Behind him, the whirl of colour evolved into a sunlit courtyard with a fountain playing, and around the perimeter, pillars like palm-trees marking off a cool shaded cloister. *Palermo:* magnet, at the dawn of the thirteenth century, for the greatest minds from every point of the compass, be they Christian, Muslim or Jew.

Into the courtyard came crowding men (and women too) of every hue and build and style of dress, all different save for the stamp of questing intellect that marked their faces as it did the emperor's. Yet even among that glittering company there was one who stood apart: the emperor's astrologer and alchemist in residence, scholar of Arabic and mathematician of genius, Michael Scot. She recognized him at once, though he was much changed since she had seen him last, in his Paris days. All trace of youth was gone; he remained amazingly thin: the great energy that burned within him seemed to consume his flesh even as it formed over his bones; his extraordinary diamond eyes were clear and penetrating as ever, yet it seemed now that they searched every face in the courtyard, seeking something not to be found in any.

Presently a small, dark-haired man with a long nose drew Scot aside to the cloister, where they sat together on a bench. This, she understood, was Leonardo of Pisa, called

Fibonacci, fellow mathematician and great traveller in the Arab world; he had brought some manuscripts for his friend, which seemed to delight him greatly. As Michael Scot pored over them, smiling, Leonardo looked about him at the milling throng that surrounded the Emperor. Suddenly he caught his breath, and laying his hand on his companion's arm, bade him look up.

A young man – a youth of no more than eighteen summers – had entered the courtyard. He was very tall and golden-haired, with a powerful athletic build and a face of remarkable beauty. He moved with an easy, confident grace, looking around him curiously, but quite unabashed even in that daunting company. He, too, seemed to search each face without finding what he looked for, until at length he turned his gaze to the shadowed cloister and his eyes met Michael Scot's. It seemed to Helen that for that moment she was both Michael Scot and the young man, and she felt a door had opened between their two minds – no, more than that, their very souls – and that there could never, between these two, be anything other than complete understanding.

The scene shifted, and she understood that time had moved on; the young man had become Scot's disciple, and together they worked at all manner of things, but she sensed that for both of them, only one thing mattered. It had to do with the manuscripts that Leonardo had brought: these they studied and discussed interminably, often breaking off to consult great books and, frequently, maps. It seemed that they were searching for something, something that had once been in one place, but was now dismantled and dispersed. Messengers were sent out with merchants sailing from the port; from time to time others came back, bringing news, or occasionally small packages. A large map now hung in the room where they worked, studded all over with coloured tassels. Sometimes, when a package arrived, one might be removed; if it was news that came, an entry was made in a huge leatherbound book, and a tassel might be shifted to another point on the map.

Now it seemed that much time had passed: the young man had grown to maturity; his master had begun to look old. The quest went on, unceasingly, but now with an urgency that had not been there before; Helen sensed that it had become a race, one that Michael Scot was losing. In the glances that the two men exchanged over the maps and documents, Helen read discord for the first time – the younger man urged the older on a course he was reluctant to follow. She sensed a weariness in Scot, a desire to be gone, that was checked only by his affection for the younger man and his reluctance to be parted from him.

At length, it seemed, the younger man had his way: preparations were made, and they removed from their rooms in the palace to a remote cottage on a hillside. There was a curious scene in the Cathedral at Palermo: at the consecration, Scot doffed an iron cap he had taken to wearing, and immediately seemed to be struck down: the disciple, stooping beside his master, held up a small stone that seemed to have struck him. The crowd shrank back, blessing themselves, exchanging fearful glances; the senseless body of the great man was hurried away. Swiftly there followed images of mourning and funeral: Michael Scot was dead.

This is a ruse, thought Helen, an excuse to remove him from the public scene. Sure enough, the next scenes showed Scot installed in a room at the cottage. Something about the room put Helen in mind of that other room in Paris on a Christmas Day long ago: she felt a sense of mounting tension and anxiety. The young man appeared, accompanied by a girl of perhaps ten or twelve. Heavy glances were exchanged between the two men: determination on the disciple's part, powerful reluctance on Scot's. The girl, sensing the tension, began to weep. Scot called her to him: he sat up in the bed and laid a hand on her cheek. She was a pretty girl, with long dark wavy hair and large dark eyes. It seemed to Helen that superimposed on this scene was another, a thin boy on the edge of a green dell taking leave of a similar dark, grave-faced girl: *and so you are going away, Michael – to Paris?*

Helen saw that behind the girl's back the young man stood with a towel over his arm and a silver basin in his hand: his other hand held a long, thin-bladed knife. Scot looked into the girl's face and stroked her cheek, smiling a little sadly; then he looked at his disciple and shook his head. The other – knife already poised – looked uncomprehending, then angry. He made to carry on regardless, but Scot bent his gaze on him in a sudden fury. Lightning seemed to dart from his brilliant eyes: the younger man staggered back, sinking to his knees; the knife fell from his hand; the basin rang on the stone floor.

Now Scot and the young man, robed in white, sat facing each other in two tall chairs like thrones, their knees almost touching. The girl attended them, bringing various articles that she set up as Scot instructed her: two candles in tall stands, which she lit; a great book, which she placed on a lectern at one side. Helen saw that the two chairs and the rest were all placed inside a double circle drawn on the floor, inscribed with various symbols. Finally, the girl set a small brazier across from the book: when she lit it, the coals burned blue and green and purple, giving off a heavy fragrance. As a last act, she went and closed the shutters, then retired from the room.

Presently there came a deep groaning like the very lowest note on an organ: the stone-flagged floor vibrated in resonance. The candles flared up an instant, then guttered till their flames were feeble blue points; the glow of the brazier grew more intense, bathing the two men in an ever-changing array of colours. Scot and his disciple, hands now palm to palm, gazed intently into each other's eyes. The disciple's face wore a look of growing wonder and delight: his eyes were wide, receptive. Scot's look was one of fierce concentration: he strained forward in his seat, eyes blazing. All the while the deep note grew in power and intensity, until it seemed that the whole room shook with it, to the point that everything must dissolve and become part of everything else, yet still it grew, mounting to an unbearable climax –

Then came a great, crashing chord, with a long reverberation fading into silence.

The door opened and someone entered the room and went to the shutters. Light flooded into the space. Helen saw first that the girl at the window was older now, nearer her own age; then she saw that the room, apart from the area within the circle, was empty – of the bed, the table, the various pieces of furniture, there was not a trace: only a thick layer of fine dust on the floor that whirled up as the shutters opened and hung in the shaft of light in tiny brilliant points. The sunshaft fell directly on the centre of the room, where within the circle, the two chairs still stood, and in them, what might have been two men; for Michael Scot seemed little more than a shell, a delicate transparent husk, with features faded like an old photograph. Even as Helen watched, the husk dissolved into a cloud of what seemed fine smoke and the chair was empty. The disciple, opposite him, seemed solid enough, sitting upright like the statue of some Egyptian Pharaoh, eyes closed, his hands on his knees.

The girl came from the window and stood by the chair and looked at the remaining man, wondering. Timidly, she laid a hand on his, then touched his cheek: there was no response. Then slowly, very slowly, the eyes began to open: it seemed to Helen that she was the girl, standing there so close, watching the lids lift slowly; and she did not know if it was her own heart that she felt give a leap or the girl's, when she saw that the eyes which looked out at her – looked out, but saw nothing – were the diamond-clear eyes of Michael Scot.

In the same room, the same figure sat in the same chair, though it had been moved now to face out the window, so that Helen could see only the curve of a shoulder and an arm. Around it, the room had been refurnished, decorated: it showed all the signs of family habitation. The door opened, and a child entered, a curly-headed little thing of three or four. The child ambled about the room, then came at length to a halt in front of the figure in the chair, at which it gazed with the solemn candour of the very young. It gazed as at an object known always as part of its life, part of this room. Presently, a flicker of curiosity crossed the young face, and the child thrust its head forward to see better, its tongue protruding slightly between its lips: then all at once it laughed, and went skipping from the room.

It returned presently pulling a woman by the hand, evidently its mother. She wore the rather harassed look of a busy parent interrupted in her daily round. Helen searched her face for some resemblance to the girl of earlier scenes, but could find none. The woman, too, scrutinized the seated figure, a puzzled frown on her face; then she gave the child some instruction, and it skipped off gleefully. The child returned with a woman full of years, clad all in black, bent and walking with the aid of a stick – its grandmother, perhaps; or great grandmother, more likely. She took her slow way towards the window, and when the light fell on her face for the first time, smoothing away the wrinkles, Helen realised with a shock that this, grown old, was the girl whom she had last seen opening the shutters, the girl who, in her long-distant youth, had attended Michael Scot and his companion.

The old woman held out a hand to the seated figure, and the figure reached out to her and grasped it; then it rose to its feet as the child and its mother gazed astonished. As the man turned in the light, Helen saw that he was scarcely changed, apart from a vigorous golden beard: he stood as tall and handsome as ever. Bending over the ancient grandmother, he took both her hands, and kissed her on the cheek.

The final scene was one of parting: the disciple, garbed for the road, stood at the door of the cottage; there, to see him off, was a great assortment of people of all ages, and by their looks, of the same family. Seated amidst them in the place of honour was the old woman, watching with an expression of mingled wonder, pride and sadness as the tall handsome man she had first seen when she was barely a child made his way, unchanged, down the white dusty road, a satchel on his shoulder, to renew his interrupted quest.

At the bend in the road he turned to make a last farewell, and the old old woman spoke a word that hung there in the clear bright air, his name:

Albanus.

19
A Secret Rendezvous

Helen woke the next morning with the tantalizing recollection that she had dreamed vividly, but of what, she had no clear remembrance. She was surprised to find the blue book by her pillow: had she been reading that before she went to sleep? Without another thought, she tucked it back in the pocket of her bag.

Jake did not emerge from his bedroom until she was on the point of going out – but the sight of him standing there in the doorway, so dishevelled and barely half awake, touched her heart: she kissed her fingers, then put them to his lips.

– *A bientôt!* see you outside the Pompidou Centre at – what? Eleven.

She gave him the blessing of her smile, and was gone. Jake gazed after her, still in a dream, his fingers to his lips. What had made her do that?

After he had eaten his breakfast and dressed, he was so restless, pacing the flat, trying to read and jumping up after two minutes, humming snatches of song to himself, that Agnès eventually threw her hands up in exasperation.

– *Mon Dieu*, can you not stay still for a minute? Look, it is a beautiful morning – why don't you go out for a walk? Otherwise you will drive me mad!

She said it sternly enough, but she could not help smiling at Jake's back, and shaking her head at the folly of young love.

Helen walked briskly, glad that she had decided to come on her own: instead of being one of a pair of teenage kids, she was now a solitary young woman making her way purposefully through the most romantic city in the world. She could imagine people looking at her as she passed, wondering who she was and where she was going. Around her, Paris was emerging into sunlight – the pavements steamed; café proprietors, with a cautious survey of the clearing sky, dared to pull in their awnings and set out chairs and tables; pedestrians confronted the trying question of whether to keep their raincoats on and what to do with their now unnecessary umbrellas. Helen felt her heart lift with the sheer exuberance of being abroad in a great metropolis: Paris in the Spring! And here she was, on her way to a secret assignation (well, secret from Jake, anyway) with a mysterious stranger!

Her father's instructions had been simple: try and find out who might be behind Negulescu, but give away as little as possible – it would be a bit like playing chess, Helen supposed. She was good at chess.

He was sitting waiting at a window table when she arrived and waved to her through the glass with a welcoming smile. Inside, the café was furnished in a severe industrial style, with a lot of metal surfaces, stainless steel and brushed aluminium predominating: the floor was a rather queasy light green. Raeburn stood gallantly and offered her his chair, squeezing round to the other side of the table to seat himself with his back to the window. As she sat down, a little flushed from walking, brushing aside a stray tendril of hair, she wondered what people would think, seeing the two of them together: not father and daughter; he was too young for that, she thought – uncle and niece, maybe? Lovers, perhaps? She smiled at the thought, at once absurd, yet, to an onlooker's eye, quite possible.

– I hope your father is all right? inquired Raeburn solicitously.

A waiter brought coffee and a chocolate croissant.

– He's fine, thanks, mumbled Helen, caught in mid-mouthful.

– He didn't look at all well – I was worried that something I said may have upset him. I'm afraid I was rather excited, yesterday.

He seemed less so today, but for all his relaxed appearance, Helen sensed an underlying tension. She helped the *chocolatine* down with some coffee, then said,

– As a matter of fact, there was something you said –

– About the crystal? interrupted Raeburn.

Helen took a sip of coffee, and said, in what she hoped was a casual manner

– Not that. (was it her fancy, or did he seem disappointed?) It was what you said about metempsychosis – you know, soul-projection – using people as emissaries, that kind of thing.

– It *was* rather a grisly tale, he conceded.

162

– I don't suppose, said Helen – hoping to sound like someone casually continuing the conversation – that there's anyone can do that kind of thing nowadays?

– Well, as a matter of fact, began Raeburn, briskly, there is certainly one man – then he hesitated a moment, looking at her, struck by some significance in her question. One man at least who certainly could…

Helen, dabbing up some crumbs of chocolate, tried to appear unconcerned, but she did not like the look on Raeburn's face, which reminded her of her father when he was pretending to pay attention to her but really trying to work something out at the back of his head. An inspiration struck her:

– This one man – it wouldn't be Aurelian Pounce, by any chance?

Because of course it couldn't be; but it might dupe Raeburn into revealing the name, and convince him that she was just being idly curious.

– Aurelian Pounce? said Raeburn. I know the name, of course – anyone who takes an interest in occult matters has heard of Aurelian Pounce. And his death caused quite a stir of course – *presumed* death, I should say, since no body was ever found – though you'd know more about it than I would, having been there – actually *in at the death*, one might even say.

He shot her a meaningful glance: Helen began to think it had not been such a clever move after all, to mention Pounce. Raeburn went on

– Of course, what everyone wondered was what he could have been up to at Ruggiero da Montefeltro's villa – they knew it had to be something to do with the painting, because that was found in the boot of his car – but what?

He stirred his coffee dreamily, gazing in front of him.

– I was so sure it was the crystal, he mused, but after yesterday...

Time seemed to Helen to slow down: she was aware of looking desperately at Raeburn's face, trying somehow to stop his thought processes just by staring at him, while at the same time she was thinking, I've blown it, I've done exactly the opposite of what Dad wanted, and I've not even learned the name – Raeburn was leaning towards her across the table, a genial smile on his face, covering her hands with his own. He was nodding his head slowly, watching everything fall into place.

– I really have to thank you, my dear, for a most *illuminating* conversation – it has opened whole new possibilities of thought – but fair's fair: I must give you something in exchange – the name your father sent you to find out, perhaps?

He shot a glance at Helen, who was by now too miserable to any attempt any concealment: she nodded, ruefully.

– *Draganu*, he calls himself – and for your father's information, he is the foremost adept in Europe: Aurelian Pounce was a mere dilettante meddler by comparison.

Helen managed a smile – at least I got what I came for, she thought, but god knows what I've given away. As she sat gazing intently at Raeburn's face, trying to fathom his thought, a shadow fell across the table from outside: Helen looked up, pulling her hands from under Raeburn's the instant before she realised it was precisely the wrong thing to do.

There, standing openmouthed at the window, was Jake.

He froze, an expression of anguish on his face, and for that moment, all Helen could do was stare back at him – then he turned away, and she sprang to her feet, upsetting the chair with a clatter on the floor. By the time she reached the door, he was halfway down the street. She called after him, but her shout was drowned by the guttural exhaust note of a powerful sports car moving off somewhere behind her. A black Maserati swept past, then slowed to a halt as it drew level with Jake, and, as Helen watched in astonishment, he looked up as if someone had called him. The passenger door swung open, he hesitated for a moment, then, without looking back, he climbed in and the car sped off, accelerating rapidly through the gears.

20
Dead Man Walking

– Mummy, what's wrong with that man's face? piped the clear voiced child.

– Hush, darling, said her mother.

She smiled apologetically at her fellow passengers, who, because she was pretty (as was the child) smiled back, indulgently, and hid their faces behind their magazines and newspapers: because of course the child was right – there was something very wrong with that man's face.

It had the colour and texture of grey putty. So unnatural did it look that it was easier to suppose it a mask, or some sort of bizarre face-paint. The eyes bulged out as though being pressed from behind, suggesting great strain; the mouth worked constantly, like a cow chewing the cud. A thin dribble of saliva ran down from one corner. His left hand, of the same leaden colour, hung slackly from his sleeve. It twitched. His right hand was thrust in his pocket; he carried a raincoat in the crook of his arm. His clothes had a crumpled look: he might have spent the night in them. The uniformed official in charge of the waiting room, feeling the eyes of the passengers on him, took a step towards the man, but then thought better of it and stood, rocking on the balls of his feet, in a torment of indecision. The grey man lurched heavily to a vacant space and slumped himself into a seat, throwing the coat on the table in front of him. The effort seemed to have exhausted him: he sat for a time, hands turned palm upwards at his sides, fingers twitching. The uniformed official relaxed and busied himself with small tasks that had suddenly become urgent to him.

– Mummy, that man's smoking now! said the clear-voiced child.

Her mother shushed her again, but this time, since the signs were perfectly clear and in three languages, she ventured a disapproving stare at the man for his breach of etiquette. What she saw made her recoil; she lunged instinctively to cover her child's eyes.

The man was indeed smoking: a thick curl of greasy smoke was emanating from his midriff. His eyes were turned down towards it, as he struggled to comprehend what was happening to him. As the hovering official watched horrorstruck, there came a soft *whoof!* and a sheet of blue-green flame flared up from the man's belly, which seemed to open like a hole burned in paper. For a moment the man continued to stare, slack-jawed, then he folded forward like a puppet with its strings cut. His head struck the table with a loud clunk. Someone screamed; the official, hurrying forward at last, took off his jacket and covered the twisted body.

****

– Well, I've seen dead and I've seen dead, said the big red-bearded ambulance-man, and man, that is *dead*.

Having delivered himself of this gnomic utterance, he busied himself with transferring the twisted grey body from the waiting room seat to the wheeled stretcher.

– What about the coat? said the stationmaster. Had that when he came, did he, George?

George, the waiting room official, nodded his head mournfully. He had been reunited with his jacket, but he seemed reluctant to put it on, examining it instead at arm's length, as though there was something about it that he distrusted.

– We'd best take it then, said the other ambulance attendant.

In contrast to his colleague, he was a small meek man, with a gentle, rather melancholy face. He gathered up the coat and followed the trolley with its sheeted burden out of the room to the waiting vehicle.

The ambulance nosed its way into the London traffic without the aid of lights or sirens: there was no hurry, after all – the patient's condition was unlikely to deteriorate.

– Now this one, said the red-bearded man, who was also the local union representative, is for the mortuary porter to deal with.

– How so? said the other, with a pretence of interest.

– 'Cause that's the agreement: a stiff 'un is mortuary work – strictly speaking we shouldn't even be picking them up – they've a van for that. Now a DOA is different – if they're alive when we get 'em, we treat 'em as such until the doctor says otherwise. But if they're dead – well, like I say, mortuary porter's work. We already done 'em a favour bringing it in, so we leave it to them to unload.

– That sounds fair enough, said the other.

They were making excruciatingly slow progress, standing for long periods then crawling forward for a hundred yards or so.

– At this rate we'll be due our break when we get in, said red-beard.

There was a chorus of hooting and flashing lights from behind.

– Some people, drawled redbeard philosophically, some people just ain't got the *patience*.

He wound down the window, leaned out, and bellowed his message to the world:

– SOME PEOPLE JUST AIN'T GOT THE PATIENCE!

– There's a joke there, maybe, said the mild one. You know – "patience" and "patients."

The other stared blankly, uncomprehending.

– Never mind, said the mild one.

He turned to look out the window, to be startled moments later by a loud guffaw.

– No, that's good, that is! Couldn't see it at first – we're the ones what's got the patients! Very good! – though it's hardly true in this case, I suppose.

The traffic began to move again, more rapidly than before. Soon they were nearing the hospital: the red-bearded one had radioed ahead to ensure the attendance of the mortuary porter. They could see him as they drove in, leaning on his trolley with a glum expression.

– What you have to drag me all the way up here for then? he began, as soon as the ambulance crew emerged. Should be on my break, I should.

– As should we, brother, said redbeard. But seeing as how this here is no DOA but a genuine stiff as collected, it falls to you to be dealt with, and not to us. Come along, Cyril!

– Actually, me name's Dave, confided the mild one to the mortuary porter, with a sympathetic shrug.

The two men had just reached the entrance doors when they were startled by an irate shout. They turned to see the mortuary porter striding towards them, rattling his trolley in front of him and turning the air blue with oaths.

– What you think this is? April the f-ing first? Think I got time for f-ing practical jokes?

– Calm down, calm down! said the mild man, interposing himself. What's the matter?

– What's the matter? What's the f-ing matter? I'll tell you what's the f-ing matter –

He poised himself to deliver some devastating riposte, but seemed unable to summon the right words; after some futile scrabbling – as if he might pluck them from the air – he said,

– O, go and looking your f-ing selves – I've wasted enough time on you as it is.

He stalked off, battering the swing doors open with his trolley. The two ambulance-men exchanged glances and made their way to the back of their vehicle, where the rear doors stood wide.

It was entirely empty, apart from a crumpled bundle on the floor.

– He's gone away without his coat, said the mild one.

*

The assistant in the chemist's shop was not amused. If it had been a schoolboy, well, she might have expected that kind of thing from schoolboys but this was a grown man, and not a young man either. He had been standing with his back to her and she couldn't help noticing the state of his clothes, it looked like he'd spent the night in them, and the smell – well no, it wasn't that kind of trampy smell at all, it was quite different, but every bit as unpleasant – a sweetish sort of smell, a bit like, well, she didn't like to say... and then he had turned round. That face! My God, it was like some sort of grey paint, all over – and the eyes, all red-rimmed and bloodshot – it had to be some sort of theatrical make-up, though what on earth he thought he was up to, at that time in the morning, God alone knows! She supposed it was meant for some kind of joke, but she certainly wasn't laughing. Then that way he had rummaged on the shelves like he couldn't properly control his movements, and had knocked all that stuff to the floor. She had yelled at him then, but took good care to stay behind the counter all the same. Had he taken something? Probably – it was hard to tell, what with the mess on the floor – face powder, lipsticks, foundation cream all over the place. She certainly wasn't going after him to find out, she was glad to see the back of him, stumbling about like that – you'd think he was drunk, took him three attempts to get through the door. Mentally ill, she was inclined to think, on reflection.

*

   – Was he wearing make-up or what? said the girl at the ticket desk to her mate.

The man with the orangey-pink face and garish red lips

171

lurched away in the direction of the platforms.

  – Hope that ticket was what he wanted. It's kind of hard when they don't speak. Look at this!

She passed across the crumpled rag of paper that the man had thrust at her. On it was scrawled, in pencil, the one word: Paris.

*

In Paris it had rained, but now the sun shone, making the pavements steam. The child tugged impatiently at her mother's arm to look, Mummy, look at that! But Mummy was too busy chatting to her friend, so the little girl had to be content to gaze backwards as she was dragged along, round eyes fixed on the strange figure that had to be a statue even though it had proper clothes on and was under a tree which was not where you put statues usually, because it was so still and real people's faces weren't like that, all streaked like paint that had run. She was still watching it intently when they reached the edge of the little park, and she gave a gasp of surprise when it lurched out from under the shelter of the tree and walked stiffly away, as if the rain had made its joints rusty.

  – Mummy, mummy! The statue moved!

  – Did it dear? that was nice!

And her mother smiled at her friend without looking back. So imaginative they were, at that age!

21
Hold-up at the
Hotel Continental

– Cheer up! said Gerald De Havilland. At least he told you the name, in the end!

– Only because he felt sorry for me! said Helen, slumped in a chair.

She felt a complete failure: she had made such a mess of things with Jake, and with her father's errand, though he didn't seem to think so – he was pleased, in a quiet sort of way, with the name that Raeburn had offered her, as a kind of consolation prize, as she stood in tears in the café: Draganu. A peculiar name; Romanian, she guessed. What she had been unable to convey to her father was her certainty that Raeburn had somehow inferred something from what she had said, as if she had unwittingly handed him the final piece of a jigsaw puzzle. That look on his face – barely concealed delight: like someone experiencing a revelation.

The room was half-filled with bright sunshine; the other half was in the shade created by the orange curtain drawn half-way across the balcony window, which bellied a little in the light breeze. The bed was strewn with clothes and odd bits and pieces.

– What on earth is that?

She indicated a strange sort of statue, like a child's model of a bird, with an almost globular body and an absurdly small head sticking out like the spout of a teapot; it was a vibrant golden yellow, spotted all over with black; it had a distinctly hand-made look.

– That's my guinea-fowl, said her father, with evident pride. Primitive art from Africa. Do you like it?

– Not enormously, said Helen, picking it up.

It was unusually heavy, and on closer inspection appeared to have suffered a drastic accident at some point – its body was crazed all over with hairline cracks, as though it had been shattered and stuck together again.

– Careful! said her father. It's really quite delicate. Give it here.

She saw that he was packing: there was a suitcase open on the floor; another, already packed, stood on its edge, draped with a coat.

– Are you going somewhere?

She began to ask, but the words died in her throat, because just then her father reached down and removed his coat to reveal the other suitcase.

It was one that she had seen before: shiny metal with a dimpled surface, the sort of thing photographers use to carry their cameras.

Her father registered her shock and followed her gaze.

Then their eyes met, and they looked at one another for a long uncomfortable moment. They were interrupted by a voice from the doorway.

 – I'll have that, if you don't mind.

It was Macintosh Raeburn, looking flushed and excited: he had a small black pistol in his hand, and his eyes were fixed on the shiny case.

 – Put it on the bed, please, and open it. I'd like to be sure I've got the right thing. No tricks, now.

De Havilland glared and swung the case up onto the bed. He flicked the catches open and lifted the lid.

Inside the case there was grey foam padding, into which two recesses had been cut. In the larger, right-hand one was an assembly of dark metal which looked halfway between the innards of a clock and the skeleton of an animal; in the other nestled a glittering crystal about the size of a small hen's egg.

 – Sorry to do this to you, old fellow, said Raeburn with forced heartiness. But you mustn't complain – you hardly came by it legally yourself.

He waved his gun for De Havilland and Helen to move away from the bed. As he went across to collect the case, Helen's eye was distracted by a movement behind her father; the orange curtain, which had been rising and falling with the breeze, was pulled aside, and a bizarre figure entered the room. Its face was daubed with orangey-pink make-up that had streaked and run, showing a leaden hue beneath; the mouth was smeared with lipstick; the whole was stiff and mask-like, apart from the eyes, which were horribly alive and malevolent. There was a long thin-bladed knife in its right hand. It was a moment before Helen registered it as

175

the same man who had so terrified her on the stairs outside her father's flat.

For a second, nobody moved; then Raeburn lunged for the case and scooped it up, cramming it shut; De Havilland, who had turned towards the intruder, turned back to try and stop Raeburn, and as he did so, the figure at the window swung at him with the knife, a sweeping side-swipe that caught in the folds of the coat on his arm. Helen started forward with a cry as she saw her father stagger beneath the blow: behind her, she heard the door close as Raeburn left the room, and she was left standing face to face with the man her father had killed once already.

*

Jake had lapsed into a daydream when the man came out of the hotel. For what seemed ages, they had been cruising in the black Maserati in the streets round about the Hotel Continental, the sun shining warmly through the windscreen, Zoë tense and silent at the wheel, awaiting some signal. Then her phone had rung: she listened briefly, and guided the car into the kerb some way short of the hotel, but kept its engine running. A minute or two later, the man emerged, turning away from them and heading down the street with the brisk jerky walk of someone pretending not to hurry. He was carrying a shiny steel case. Jake recognized him at once from his back view – it was the man who had been at the auction, the same one he had seen earlier this morning with Helen in the café (the recollection made him wince) – her so-called 'gentleman caller'.

As Zoë eased the car out from the kerb, Jake found

himself wondering if he was destined never to see his rival's face – perhaps he has none, he mused, still half in his dream. Then the man, instead of going straight ahead, ducked down an alley at the side of the hotel. Zoë raced the car forward and swerved in after him with a loud squeal of tyres, so that Jake, flung sideways, had to brace himself against the door and the dashboard.

The alleyway was short and quite broad, obviously meant to allow access to the row of steel dustbins arrayed down one side: above them, a fire escape zigzagged from the upper floors of the hotel in a series of stairs and platforms. Beyond that, there was a dead wall, and for a moment Jake thought the man was trapped – until he saw there was a narrow lane to one side, passable only on foot.

What happened next had a dream-like quality: as the man passed the fire escape, something large dropped on him from above, and it was a moment before Jake realised it was another man. The man with the case staggered and fell, the other on top of him, and Jake saw the glint of a knife blade raised to stab, then brought down with brutal force. Zoë raced the Maserati forward as if she meant to run them down, but instead she slewed it expertly broadside on and flung open the door. For an instant Jake was confronted by what seemed a snapshot of the two struggling men, framed in the doorway – both had raised their heads and were looking in at them, momentarily distracted.

The man on top was bizarre to look at: he seemed to be wearing some sort of face-paint, streaks of grey alternating with orangey flesh-tints; but for all that, it was the man underneath who held Jake's attention – at last, he had seen the face of his rival, and it was a face he knew, the last he would have expected to confront him in this Paris alleyway.

He gave a startled cry as Zoë reached out to snatch the case and haul it into the car, shoving it across to his lap – a sharp corner dug into his thigh – as she reached out once more and slammed the door shut.

She spun the car skilfully so that its nose was pointing out to the street, but as she completed the manoeuvre there was a heavy thump on the back and Jake turned to see the grotesque streaked face pressed against the rear window as the man scrabbled to hang on; Zoë muttered under her breath and pressed the accelerator, sending the Maserati leaping forward, then stamped on the brake so hard that it almost stood on its nose – the scrabbling figure somersaulted over the roof, appearing briefly in front of them as it bounced off the bonnet and slithered aside as Zoë accelerated once more.

It was only when they had regained the street that Jake was able to overcome his shock sufficiently to speak.

– That man – it was –

– Not now, Jake, she said soothingly.

She leaned across, encircling him with her arm, her face close to his, as though to comfort him; then he felt the firm pressure of her fingers on his neck and he lost consciousness.

22
The Contents of the Steel Case

Jake came to with a start. He was sitting in a big leather armchair in a darkened room: blinds were drawn down over the windows. It was some moments before he realised he was not alone. Sitting across from him, watching him closely, was Zoë.

– Hello, Jake. Sorry about putting you to sleep... it seemed the best thing in the circumstances: you looked to have had a terrible shock.

He sat bolt upright, disjointed scenes flashing across his memory: a distorted and discoloured face pressed against the rear window of a car; a body bouncing off the bonnet – had they run someone down? No – a body falling, no, *dropping* from a fire escape, dropping on a man with a steel case, a man they were following – it was coming to him now – two men struggling on the ground, framed in the doorway of the car, looking up at him –

– That man in the alleyway – the man who had the case –

She was watching him intently, urging him on, it seemed, towards the impossible conclusion –

– I know him: or at least, I think I do – only it can't be –

He looked at her for guidance: she gave an encouraging nod. He took a deep breath, then said, surprised at the calmness of his own voice,

– It was Mr. Macintosh, my English teacher.

Zoë watched him impassively, her chin supported on her hand.

– It just doesn't make any sense, said Jake.

Zoë looked at him a little longer, then seemed to come to a decision.

– Perhaps I can help you with that, she said.

She got up from her chair and went out of the room. Jake looked about him. It was a big room: there were windows on three walls, all with blinds drawn down. The blinds were not completely opaque – he could see that it was still bright daylight outside; through the filter of the material, it created a sort of brownish twilight within. There was not much else in the room: a table, on which stood the steel suitcase, its lid flipped open. Jake hesitated, then went over for a closer look: in the grey foam interior he could make out the familiar shape of the Alchemist's machine; alongside it was a large crystal.

He looked at it with feelings of disquiet mingled with relief: for all its failure to deliver – he laughed at himself now for his early expectations of it, that it would somehow make their fortune instantly – he could not rid himself, in its presence, of ominous feelings; perhaps that had strengthened since Stephen Langton's murder. Hence his relief, when he thought that it was now passing out of his life for good, back to whoever was its rightful owner – he guessed it would end up in a museum somewhere; who knows, maybe one day he would go there and come on it quite by accident, and that would bring him back to this moment now, in this darkened room.

Could that *really* be what all this was about? To recover an exhibit for a museum? He thought again of Zoë in the Maserati, the way she slid and spun it so expertly, the coolness and precision with which she snatched the case – ruthless, too: what heed had she paid to the fact that there, within touching distance, one man was murdering another? When she had spoken in the café about how seriously some countries took their culture and heritage, it had been in terms of striking deals, bending the law a bit to secure some article – there was nothing about dramatic snatches in broad daylight, executed with military precision; then there was that thing she had done to his neck afterwards, putting him out like a light – Helen said the same had happened to her. He began to think that Zoë must be rather more than just a field agent for some Department of Culture and Heritage.

Where was she, anyway? He made his way back to the armchair, but remained standing. There were two doors in the back wall – the left hand one Zoë had gone out, and another on the right. He was just thinking of inspecting it when it swung open, to show a figure silhouetted against the light – he was immediately reminded of something, and an instant later he knew what, when a husky voice said

– Well, hello Jake.

He stared in amazement at the dark outline, the wavy mass of blue-black hair falling about the shoulders.

– Miss Wilbright! he croaked, incredulously.

Then she stepped into the room and with a quick

movement of her arm removed the wig – and became Zoë again.

– You! But what – how –?

She laughed at his consternation, but not unkindly.

– Actually, I'm surprised you didn't notice before now – though it goes to prove what I said before about disguise being all in the context: you expect to see Gerald De Havilland's mistress in his London flat; you do not expect to be picked up by your sometime Art teacher in the middle of Paris, driving a Maserati. Any more than you expect to see your English teacher attacked in an alley beside the Hotel Continental, she added, more seriously.

– I don't understand, said Jake simply, shaking his head.

– Macintosh Raeburn – or Mr. Macintosh as you knew him – is someone we have had our eyes on for some time.

Jake noted her use of 'we' with its reassuring suggestion of some large and powerful organization.

– So much intelligence work (she noted Jake's reaction to that phrase with a small smile) depends on picking the right people to watch – the ones who will give you warning signs. Large events are always preceded by a million tiny indicators, sudden breaks in routine by people who know what's coming – the knack is to make sure you're looking in the right place. In this matter now (she nodded in the direction of the steel case) we knew that Macintosh Raeburn was one to watch. He's a writer, an obsessive who has made himself one of the leading authorities on the *Thaumatophane* – the proper name for what you think of as the Alchemist Ruggiero's machine. If there was anything at all happening in relation to it, his antennae would be the first to pick it up…so of course when Ruggiero's house collapses in mysterious circumstances, and a painting well known for its occult

182

significance is found close at hand – *The Secret of the Alchemist* – it is very interesting to us to see what our friend's reaction to it is – so when we find him joining the staff of your school, we are naturally very curious as to what he is up to...

– Actually, said Jake, he did try Helen first, but he didn't get anywhere.

– Did he now? Of course you two were the only ones whose names appeared in the newspaper reports, and I suppose Helen was closer – he actually lives in Tuscany, so we wouldn't reckon a trip to Switzerland all that unusual, but a move to Glasgow, in the guise of a teacher – that we did notice.

– So you followed him?

She smiled.

– We wanted to see where he would lead us – he wasn't the big fish, but he could be the bait that let us catch it.

– It was that Friday, wasn't it? said Jake, seeing it all now. He was asking me about Stephen Langton, and then you came in – and what did you do to me?

– Sorry about that – but I needed to know what he told you. It's a standard debriefing technique – a form of hypnotism.

– So that's how you found your way to Silk House – I told you!

Again, she smiled.

– I managed to beat Macintosh Raeburn to it, mainly by – er, delaying him on the Friday night.

The smile was a wicked one this time, and Jake recalled the rumours he had discounted about the two of them being seen out together.

– Unfortunately I did not arrive soon enough, as I told you – Stephen Langton was already dead.

Jake steeled himself to repeat the question he had asked her in the café: if it wasn't Zoë, and she was there ahead of Macintosh –

– So who did kill Stephen Langton?

– I'm almost certain now it was the man you saw in the alley today, attacking Raeburn. His name is Negulescu: he is the creature of a man named Draganu – the big fish I mentioned.

– This isn't about ancient artefacts, is it? said Jake – feeling ridiculous as he said it.

She didn't laugh, though: instead, she looked at him thoughtfully.

– It is about one particular ancient artefact: the *Thaumatophane*.

– What is it?

She gave an odd laugh.

– As to that, no one is quite sure – perhaps no one has ever been sure.

– But surely – whoever made it –?

– We do not know who made it, or for what purpose – what it was capable of was only gradually discovered, it seems: certainly, it was innocent enough at first, by all reports – perhaps because its users were innocent… but after a time a shadow crept over it: there was some link, apparently, between the will of its user and its operation – all this is very obscure, I have to tell you, but it seems to have been a classic example of power corrupting those who wield it – it has even been speculated that perhaps it was a sort of laser, except that it did not concentrate light, but in some way the energy of the will… a frightening thought.

– So it's a weapon, then?

She shrugged.

– It is as I said: no-one actually knows. But what cannot be used as a weapon? Sadly, there seems to be no limit to human ingenuity in that direction. It is certainly not something you would want to fall into the wrong hands.

– Meaning this man Draganu?

She nodded.

– Draganu is the last man on earth who should be allowed to gain possession of the Thaumatophane.

– Who is he?

– As to that...she gave a grim smile, as though the task of describing him was beyond her. Nowadays, he passes for a retired business man with a taste for art collecting – he was in very deep with the old regime in Romania, but he has money on a scale that can buy general amnesia, so no one mentions that now. He has been many things in his time, but his real reputation is as a practitioner of Black Magic – he is reckoned by those who know to be the foremost adept in Europe. He is the sort that flourishes close to power – it would surprise you, perhaps, to know how many leaders – not just benighted dictators, either – are fascinated by the occult – it is the promise of certainty that lures them, the lust for control...Draganu has had the ear of many prominent men down the years, in politics and business... he is an extremely dangerous man

Jake glanced over at the steel case, more relieved than ever that its contents were passing out of his life.

– You'll be glad you got your hands on that, then, he said, nodding towards it.

She gave a rueful laugh.

– I was indeed, until I discovered my mistake.

Jake looked at her.

– The machine is a fake, a mock-up fashioned from resin.

The Stone is the cut-glass dummy from the Auction room.

– But then – who?

– The man who has had them all along, it seems – your girlfriend's father, Gerald De Havilland.

Jake felt he had just scrambled clear of a pit, only to have the ground give way beneath him, so that slowly, helplessly, he was sliding back in

– Which is why I would like to retain your services a little longer, Jake, to intercede on my behalf, to see if we can prevent Gerald De Havilland from committing the ultimate folly of selling the machine to Draganu.

Jake saw himself, turning up with Zoë to a meeting somewhere in Paris with Helen's father – and Helen would be there too, wondering at Jake's part in all this, amazed to hear the real story from his lips.

– Yes, certainly, he said.

– There is one complication, however.

She led him over to the window and raised the blind dramatically. There, parked on a broad expanse of sunlit grass and looking like nothing so much as a piece of modern sculpture, was a small aeroplane. It was remarkably beautiful, of rather unusual design, with a pair of tiny wings on either side of the nose and its main wings far back on the fuselage near the tail. He thought at first it was a jet, then he saw that the engines were back-to-front, with the propellers at the rear.

– De Havilland and his daughter are at Orly airport, bound for Istanbul. If we are to catch them, we must fly.

– Cool! said Jake.

***

Jake felt like pinching himself as they took off – it was like something in a film: spurned by his girlfriend, the hero gives chase in a private plane piloted by a beautiful woman: it was all he could do to keep the grin off his face. To do Helen credit, she had in fact left a note with her cousin Agnès of where they were going, and had even left the cost of the airfare, but it gave Jake great pleasure to be able to say to Agnès over the phone that it was all right, he would make his own arrangements in that respect. Then he gave himself over to watching the French countryside spread out like a map below, but as they climbed higher he found the unearthly beauty of the sunlit cloudscapes monotonous after a time, and fell asleep.

When he woke again, the scene from the cockpit window was spectacular. A huge circular gap had opened like a whirlpool in the clouds, directly ahead of them; the main bank was dark and threatening, but at its edge the rays of the declining sun caught and kindled the ragged streamers of cloud into fiery tongues. It's like the descent to Hell, thought Jake, as the plane angled down towards the whirling gap.

Suddenly they were plummeting earthwards and only Jake's seat belt stopped him from hitting the roof as the plane dropped away beneath him; beside him he could see Zoë pulling back on the throttle and he felt, rather than heard, the engines spooling down in response; his eyes were stretched painfully wide, and his mouth too, so that his jaw hurt – he thought he must be screaming, but he could not hear himself.

Then it was all over: it could only have lasted seconds, though it had seemed an age. The plane stabilized, and Zoë looked across at him, as he sat white and shaken, hands clutching the armrests.

– Sorry about that – an air pocket. Are you all right?

Jake, wide-eyed with terror and unable to speak, nodded his head – though it wasn't true at all: he was far from being all right. As the plane fell, instead of his life flashing before his eyes, a single thought had bobbed to the surface of his mind, like the first piece of wreckage signalling disaster: *Macintosh came in November.*

Then another joined it: *Miss Wilbright was there after the October break.*

From that, the inexorable conclusion: she couldn't have been following Macintosh: she was there before him.

It was Jake she had been after all along.

23
Helen in Byzantium

Helen stretched out on the hotel bed. If she sat up, she could see through the filmy curtains the waters of the Bosphorus, with many great ships passing to and from the Black Sea and Istanbul. She had purposely postponed the delights of Istanbul till the morning, knowing she was too tired to do them justice, and her father had been happy to do so – he had business of his own to attend to. He was away now, visiting a mysterious Mr. Palaeloglu; he had been vague about when he would be back. Presumably this was the client to whom her father hoped to sell the machine: she was quite happy for him to stay away all night if it meant that they were finally rid of the accursed thing. In the meantime, she felt at something of a loose end: she did not want get up, but at the same time she was not inclined to sleep – perhaps if she read something?

The thought brought with it the recollection of Sophie's

book, and a curious sensation: she felt sure she had actually looked at it already – perhaps on more than one occasion – but she could recall nothing of what it had been about; yet at the same time she had no doubt that as soon as she opened it, it would all come back to her. The familiarity began with the curious tingling, like a mild electric shock, that ran through her fingers as soon as she touched the book. Yes, that had happened before. And what came next? There was something peculiar about the language it was written in – she could not recall precisely what. She opened the book at random and without looking ran her fingertips over the page.

She was in a high place, looking upward. The sky was a heavy, uniform grey: flakes of snow filtered down from it. It was cold, but there was heat coming from somewhere below. She felt an acrid vapour prick her nostrils: it made her want to cough. Was that fog, or wisps of smoke? She was bound securely and could not move her limbs or body – only her head was free. She knew without shifting her gaze down that she was on some sort of platform on one side of a square enclosed on the other three sides with buildings. The square was filled with people; more crowded the balconies, from which long banners hung limp in the cold air.

She had a sense of waiting, as for a decisive moment – a period of calm before some swift and deadly movement, like a swordthrust.

She looked down, and there he was, a tall youth in a bonnet of striking blue, gazing back with a look of frightened rapture. All else faded to grey: there was only the youth gazing helpless, wide-eyed. It seemed to Helen that she was drawn out of the place where she was and traversed space in some way she could not comprehend: she had become a concentrated beam of energy that flowed towards the young man's eyes; at the same time she was aware of all that was around her – the platform behind her (which she saw now was built around a smoking pyre); the huge crowd that filled the square, the banner-hung buildings, the snow-laden sky overhead: all this she somehow saw all at once, from no single viewpoint, yet all perfectly in place. Time stretched out: what she knew to be a moment – she saw one man in the crowd in the very act of sneezing, his eyes straining forward, his lips flapping slackly with incredible slowness – was like an age: she felt she was in a separate time altogether, or perhaps not in time at all, and might stay to look at everything at her leisure.

She felt an immense sense of liberation, of being at one with the universe, as if she could reach the farthest extremes of it in an instant; then came a jarring shock, like colliding with a wall – there was an instant of blackness and confusion, then she found herself looking up at the scaffold and the pyre, where she could see the figure of a man tied to the stake, slumped lifeless in a shroud of smoke – the image held steady for a brief space, then dissolved into shimmering mist.

She was sitting in a garden in a hot place in the shade of a tree. She had the sense that time had passed, a great deal of time, without anything happening. She felt cut off from the world she could see – no sound from it reached her, nor any smell – she seemed encased in a chamber of thick pure glass. A servant came bearing a tray, an old woman dressed in black with a child clutching her skirts; she set the tray on the table. On it were a silver cup, a flask of red wine, a loaf of bread and some cheese. With weary patience the woman filled the cup and began to tear the bread into small pieces as the child watched, round-eyed. Then she sliced a sliver of cheese, which she rolled up in some bread, then placed the morsel in the hand that lay palm upward on the table.

Helen observed the hand with detached curiosity, noticing it for the first time. Then she realised it belonged to her, or to whoever it was whose eyes she was seeing out of. The woman folded the fingers round the bread and cheese and gently lifted the hand; after she had begun the action, the hand continued it, lifting it to a mouth which accepted the food and began to chew it. Helen was aware of the sensation of eating only as a movement of muscles: she could taste nothing. After a few more morsels of bread, the cup of wine was raised, with the woman's assistance, and Helen felt the liquid in her mouth and throat but nothing more. It was apparent to her that this was something often repeated. She felt an enormous weariness and frustration.

She sat under the same tree in the same garden in the everlasting heat but now it was the child, grown to a woman of mature years, who attended her with the same cup and tray. She paid no more heed to the person she was feeding than if it had been a statue: endless repetition of the same activity had worn away any sense of human fellowship. When the ritual was complete, Helen expected her to gather up the tray and go, but instead she sat on, contemplating her charge with a dark, thoughtful stare. Her face wore the look of one working herself up to some crucial decision: after a time she rose from her chair and began to pace about. Finally, she moved away, not in the direction of the house but towards a small door let into the high wall that surrounded the garden. This she unbarred and opened; at once, three men came in.

They had the look of sailors about them, and more – an air of dangerous swagger that suggested the corsair. One handed the serving woman a bag of coins; the other two came on towards the tree. Helen saw that they carried cutlasses; one had a coil of rope. She felt herself seized by the elbows and raised to her feet: one of the men leaned into her face and spoke words, but she could tell only by the movement of his mouth – no sound came to her. The blade of the cutlass pricked her throat; behind, the other man was busy with the rope. The woman, conversing at the gate with the man who had given her the money, glanced nervously over her shoulder at the house, and gestured to them to hurry.

Now she was in a boat, and it was night: she lay at full length on her back in some sort of shallow hold, staring upwards. The stars glittered in a velvet sky. As she watched them she felt an inward stirring, like something long asleep rousing from slumber: the sense of infinite weariness altered to alertness. She was aware of a huge, sustained effort of will, of colossal energy long pent-up at last released and directed to a particular end: she feared that the feeble body would not have the strength to contain it – it shook and juddered, as though convulsed by an electric current. Suddenly, she sat upright.

She could hear the sea.

In a hall hewn out from a great sea-cave a man sat on a throne of barbaric splendour carved from ivory and painted wood and studded with coarse-cut gems. The throne was huge, but the man who sat there filled it to capacity: he was conceived on a monumental scale, broad in the shoulder and deep in the chest, his massive head framed with flowing blue-black locks and an enormous shaggy beard, his huge fleshy nose like the curved beak of some predatory bird, his wide-spaced eyes dark and cruel. He had the look of a man with monstrous appetites, but he was no brute: his dark gaze was filled with cunning intelligence. He seemed well satisfied with the prisoner his men had brought.

Presently he rose and began to pace up and down, stroking his long beard and casting sudden sidelong glances in the hope of catching some unguarded response. After a time he began to speak, in a confiding tone.

– Those fools in Ferrara: it was a husk they burnt. They did not see the spirit fly or guess where it went. But I saw, I guessed – though at first I did not believe it possible. I was a boy then, a chance visitor from abroad, trailing at my father's heels, learning the merchant's trade. What fate led me to that square? Something drew me. Albanus – the greatest wizard of the age, they said; in him, the spirit of Michael Scot yet lives. Those were only names then, but I wondered at them, longed to know more. Fifty years I have spent, from that day to this, in quest of you, and in preparation for this moment. Study is not congenial to me: I am a man of action. I learned early that pirates had superior business methods to merchants like my father: why pay for what you can take by main force and superior will? My name now is feared the length and breadth of the Mediterranean; but all that while I have led a double life, spending my wealth on books, making the acquaintance of men of learning – how the good scholars of Bologna and Salamanca would tremble if they knew with whom they dealt! (He gave a great shout of laughter, which echoed round the cave: his striding became more agitated; he waved his arms as he spoke.) But now, but now we come to it! Now at last the tree bears fruit! (He stopped, suddenly, and brought his face up very close.) Do not think that I am a fool: I know my limits. I cannot hope to overmaster you, for all my strength of will. If we join, it can only be by your consent. The choice is yours – fifty years you have been a prisoner in a body you can do nothing with, its mind shattered beyond recovery. I offer you freedom, in exchange for partnership: will you take it?

Helen felt a strong discord within, as of two jarring notes sounded simultaneously:

No!
Yes!

For a moment two massive forces opposed, perfectly balanced – on one side, a great distrust and suspicion, an unwillingness to relinquish the least particle of control, and underlying it a deep well of sadness, as one who regrets a wrong turn taken long, long ago – the image of a sunlit dell hovered before her, like a faded picture: *and so you are going away, Michael – to Paris?* On the other side, she felt that the suspicion and distrust were acknowledged, but overwhelming them like a gigantic wave of the sea was a huge yearning for action, for life, as a prisoner must feel when after long captivity he has a glimpse of freedom – *we must take this chance, come what may – there is no other.*

For a space the two contended equally, neither giving ground; then slowly, slowly, regret gave way to the thirst for life.

Helen jerked awake, knowing only that the instant before her head must have been drooping in sleep. Where was she? Wide eyed, she took in the unfamiliar surroundings: of course, it was a hotel room, on the Black Sea: they had come to Istanbul.

She stood up and stretched, noting that beyond the window the day had advanced to evening. Her head felt muzzy and confused: how long had she been asleep? She opened the French windows and a cool breath of air blew in from the balcony. It would be pleasant to take a stroll along the sea-front before bed.

Outside it was a magical night: the stars overhead seemed much bigger and brighter than she was used to; from somewhere in the direction of the shore came the smell of fish frying, and a clear voice – a woman's – said, in an Australian accent, "Y'know, sometimes at work I used to dream of doing this." Out at sea, navigation lights bobbed, a ruby and an emerald marking the entrance to a channel. Helen breathed in and gave a deep sigh of content. Although it was late, there were still quite a few people about, scattered about the street, lounging in doorways or conversing in animated knots. Drawn up by the kerb a little way from the hotel entrance was a huge old car. It was unusually tall, and had a tiny rear window like a coach, but the glass was dark; blinds were drawn down over the long windows of the passenger compartment.

It looked like the sort of car once used by British Royalty: she could imagine it sweeping through the gates of Buckingham Palace. Helen walked along its length, admiring the interplay of curves and lines: the sweep of the running board, with the circle of the spare wheel; the domed back of the giant headlamp, the flat ribbed top of the radiator. A striking thing was the lack of brightwork: parts you might have expected to be chrome or brass were dark polished metal, which lent the car a sinister look, accentuated by its horn which consisted of a long serpentine tube ending in a gleaming black trumpet shaped like a snake's head, jaws gaping. She ran her fingers over the cold polished metal. Jake would have liked to see this, she thought, with a flicker of sadness. All at once she found herself hoping fervently that he would come, and that when he was here it could be as it was in Florence – just the two of them, a boy and a girl enjoying themselves in a wonderful city, with none of these ponderous layers of feeling and complication that had troubled them in Paris.

As she walked on past the car, the numbers of people seemed to increase around her – where before there had been no one, now there was a crowd, moving and jostling together. There seemed to be some kind of argument taking place, growing more heated by the moment. Voices were raised; the people who had been walking alongside stopped, spilling across the width of the pavement, blocking her way ahead. Those behind pressed on, forcing her forward into an ever-diminishing space. She heard behind her a curious sort of mechanical cough, followed by a succession of short, rhythmic hisses; wondering what it might be, she turned and saw the big black car gliding towards her, driving very close to the kerb. As it bore down on her, serpent horn gaping, the door to the rear compartment swung back, like a great hand put out to gather her up; at the same time, she felt people press close about her, lifting her onto the running board and thrusting her into the dark passenger compartment. The door swung shut and the car sped away.

24
Deep Cover

From the moment the plane touched down, Jake had been looking for some way to escape. He reckoned he had managed to pass off his agitated state on the plane as the effect of falling through the air-pocket, and Zoë did not seem perturbed by his lack of communication, or was too busy flying to notice it. As they swung in over Istanbul with its fantastic skyline of minarets and domes outlined against the deep blue evening, Jake felt he had been transported into some perilous tale from the *Arabian Nights*; even on the ground, where a more modern and prosaic life was evident in the airport buildings, the line of waiting taxis, the thronging traffic with its blaring horns, something of the slightly sinister magical quality persisted: this was a deeply *foreign* city, quite unlike Paris – there he would have felt prepared to make a run for it at any opportunity, to plunge into the crowd, duck down a side street, take his chances –

confident that he would, soon enough, be able to make contact with a world he understood, where he felt secure. But here, amid this maze of streets and narrow alleys, he had the strong sense that just beneath the modern surface lurked a quite different, ancient place – this, after all, was once Constantinople, last relic of the Roman Empire, and before that, the ancient, mysterious city of Byzantium – here, with a past that reached back twenty-seven centuries, you might step into a doorway and vanish into history.

What made things worse was the fact that Zoë was now paying him much closer attention, and seemed to have registered that something was troubling him – he tried to look cheerful and unconcerned, but wasn't making a very good job of it, as she kept looking at him, then away again, with a thoughtful expression. He tried to distract himself by looking out the window: Istanbul in the evening was a lively place, with pavement cafés full of bustle and life, the streets a throng of cars (there was much honking of horns) and on every side the ripple of neon lights, green, blue, red and white. The taxi was crawling along, and after a quick glance around, Zoë seemed to come to a decision – she said something to the driver, and a little further on, he pulled up outside a café.

– We need to talk, I think, she said, leading him to a table, then placing an order at the counter.

Jake looked up and down the street: it was a busy thoroughfare full of shops, bars and cafés, with crowds of people going in and out of them. If he ducked into a shop, what were his chances of making himself understood? A lot of the people looked like tourists – some of them must speak English, surely? Not for the first time, he found himself envying Helen her facility for languages. In the other direction there was a major crossroads – a good place to lose pursuit. If only he could get hold of a map –

– Thinking of making a run for it? said Zoë, sitting across from him.

– Eh? No, not at all, said Jake clumsily. Why should I be thinking that?

– Because you've realised that I arrived at the school before Macintosh, so I couldn't have been following him? she queried, with a smile.

Jake stared, openmouthed, unable to conceal his feelings, unable even to speak.

– Remember in London? Helen assumed I was her father's mistress; as I told you, the easiest identity to take on is the one that others have already given you. Back there, it suited you to think I was following Macintosh, so I went with that.

– And now? Jake eventually managed to croak.

– And now I'll have to tell you something different, she laughed, because that won't work any more.

The light-hearted way she said it wrong-footed Jake: it was the last thing he expected. She was sipping her coffee now, looking at him like someone coaxing a small boy out of a sulk.

– Don't take it so hard, Jake – it's not as if we were lovers! If it's any consolation, deceiving you is all in the line of work.

– So what are you now? rejoined Jake, bitterly. You've been an art teacher, then somebody's mistress, then someone from culture and heritage, and after that, some sort of secret agent –

She laughed again.

– Quite a catalogue, isn't it? Though I can tell you, that's nothing to some of the lies I've told, she said blithely, but basically, I do work in intelligence – gathering information.

– About what? demanded Jake.

– 'What' isn't the question, Jake – it's *how*. To obtain some kinds of information – the most valuable kind – you need to get close to people – very close, so that they'll tell you all their secrets without knowing who you are. I work *undercover*, Jake – and do you know that *means*? It's not about dressing up and wearing disguises, though I do my share of that – it means living a lie – and I mean *living* it – because the people you are trying to get close to would kill you if they knew who you really were. *That's* what I do, Jake.

She gave him an earnest look: Jake looked back stonily, not willing to trust her, yet.

– So who are you trying to get close to? he demanded.

She gave him a long look, weighing him up: was she deciding to tell him the truth, or just trying to work out what lie to spin him this time?

– Or can't you tell me, he sneered, because it would blow your cover?

– Would you believe me if I did? she asked.

– Try me.

She kneaded her lower lip in her teeth, deciding; then she said.

– All right: Draganu.

She paused.

– And I'm not *trying* to get close to him, I'm already there. In fact, I'm one of his most trusted lieutenants.

– What!?

– It was I who alerted him to the events at Forcalquier last summer – the unexplained destruction of Ruggiero's house, the recovery of the painting, *The Secret of the Alchemist*, close by – and of course, the disappearance of Aurelian Pounce, a well-known occultist dabbler. It was I who suggested the possibility that the Thaumatophane had been recovered, and further, that you offered the best hope of finding out more about it.

Jake stared at her, almost speechless.

– But – but *why*? he managed to croak, at last.

– So that he would put me in charge of finding it for him.

Jake looked uncomprehending.

– Draganu is an old man – much older than anyone thinks – and he is close to death. But he is an adept, and he has – she hesitated, and a look of anguish crossed her face – he has a contingency plan, a way he could cheat death… but almost the only thing that would make him postpone it would be the prospect of recovering the Thaumatophane – for that, he would delay – *has* delayed, many months already.

Jake, looking at her face, was in no doubt that she was telling the truth this time – her expression suggested some deep-rooted sorrow.

– Can you see the beauty of it, and the risk? To tempt him with the one thing he must not be allowed to get hold of, the one thing he would risk everything to obtain, even his life – and then to delay, and delay, until …

She made a gesture of finality, striking one hand off the other, the look on her face frightening in its intensity – an almost savage triumph.

– You really hate him, don't you? said Jake, shocked by her ferocity.

She looked at him with an expression that was difficult to read: anger? pain? sorrow? Then she said simply,

– He was responsible for the death of my mother.

Jake was silent for a time, digesting this. At last he said

– Was that why you volunteered?

She looked at him blankly, then seemed to come back from a faraway place.

– Volunteered, prompted Jake. For this assignment.

– O, yes, she said vaguely, then more brightly, yes, of course, that was why I did it – and it was working, too, until Macintosh Raeburn made the same deductions I had, then followed the same leads...

A chilling thought occurred to Jake.

– But if you're working for Draganu, and Draganu had Stephen Langton killed, aren't you –

– Responsible for his death? Yes, in a way I am – though I knew nothing about Negulescu's involvement until I reached Silk House that day. I think that Draganu was beginning to tire of my lack of progress –

– Does he suspect you, then? asked Jake in alarm.

– I don't think so, at least not yet – you see, I had a stroke of luck: De Havilland must already have removed the mechanism of the Thaumatophane, so Negulescu didn't get it – and I was able to tell Draganu in Paris that I was just on my way to collect it – you remember the phone call I made in the café? Then – well, you know what happened after that.

– But what would you have done – if you had got it, I mean?

– Taken my time about delivering it, I suppose – he's living on borrowed time as it is – with any luck, the combination of excitement and delay would have proved fatal.

– But what will you do now?

– Ah, she said, with a look that made Jake feel a little nervous. That was where I hoped to enlist your assistance...if

203

we could swap the crystals again, that would do the trick – the Thaumatophane is useless without the Stone. We just have to hope that Gerald De Havilland hasn't delivered it yet – though I don't see that he can have – they only arrived a little way ahead of us, and it would take time to set up the deal.

Jake took a deep breath. He tried to think clearly: could he really trust her? Her candour was persuasive – she had been quite open about deceiving him, and why; and what she was saying this time – well, it had the ring of truth about it, and she had explained a lot of things in a way that made sense –

– What do you want me to do? he asked. We've got the address of the hotel – you could just drop me off there, and I could see what I could do –

She pursed her lips and put her head on one side, weighing up what he proposed; then she shook her head decisively.

– No – too risky. We'll need to take precautions – do a bit of groundwork. If you're willing, that is?

For the look she gave him then, he would have agreed to anything.

25
Voices in the Air

When the murmuring voice ceased, Helen was awake, curiously unconcerned about where she was or how she got there: uppermost in her mind was the urgent sense that there was something she must do. She sat up.

She was in a room, not entirely dark but lit by a strong moon shining in at the window; she was in bed, and wearing an unfamiliar nightdress of heavy silk. She swung her legs over the side of the bed and felt a rug like goatskin under her feet. She padded across to the window: the rest of the floor was cool tile. She saw that the room was in an upper story: a moon-silvered roof sloped away below, and she looked out at the tops of tall trees.

Going to the door, she opened it and turned left, without hesitation. She had the familiar, tantalizing sensation of having dreamt vividly, without being able to recall the detail, yet this time it was different – this time she felt there was some strong connection between what she was doing now

– where she was going now, in fact – and what she had been dreaming; not only that, but she felt sure that all the dreams she had been having lately were about the same thing, and that if she only kept going, she would discover what it was.

The path she followed was a complicated one, through corridors striped with moonlight, with strange furniture crowding in on either side, chests and presses and carved sideboards, and on the wall the bulky outlines of animal heads jutting between cloth hangings and heavy-framed paintings; sometimes going down steps, but more often going up, and always with complete confidence. It seems I am going right to the top of the house, she thought. She felt oddly detached, as though she were watching some other girl, and was mildly curious to see where she was going.

At length she emerged into a sloping corridor that angled upwards. Bars of moonlight lay across her path; looking out, she saw that she was above the level of the roof, apparently crossing a chasm between one building and another. At the upper end of the corridor was a tall, double-leafed door, carved with curious symbols: one leaf stood slightly ajar. She faltered: there was something solemn and portentous about the door, as if the solution to some great mystery lay beyond – she felt drawn towards it, yet wary of going further. It would not have surprised her greatly to hear music – something from *The Magic Flute*, perhaps –

Instead, she heard voices – beyond the door, there was a low whispering. It had a curious, disembodied quality: it seemed to be in the air, not coming from people at all.

It ceased almost as soon as she noticed it, but she stood for some time afterwards, stock still, straining to hear. No further sound came down to her, and cautiously she walked towards the door. It was open just wide enough to let her slip through sideways.

On the other side, she was surprised to find herself in the open air: she was on the edge of a flat roof. In front of her was an extraordinary edifice, a kind of shallow dome, like an upturned saucer, supported at its perimeter by a series of open arches. Inside, a forest of slender pillars seemed wrapped in luminous fog – then she saw that there were layers of diaphanous material that caught and diffused the moonlight as they stirred in the warm night air. There was a core of soft brightness at the heart of the building, a mellow golden light, like a little moon trapped in there.

Helen stole forward under an arch and went in among the shimmering cloths. Almost at once, the whispering started again: it seemed to be in the air above her head, and came from all around, not from a single source. The floor beneath her feet was cool and pleasant: looking down, she saw that it was richly patterned, though the colours were subdued in the moonlight. Near the centre of the dome she came to a circular space, free of hangings and pillars. In the midst of it was an extraordinary canopy affair, like an elaborate tent, made up of multiple layers of the same diaphanous material: a concentration of shadow at the heart of it suggested a presence there, humped and rounded like a giant beehive. There was a whiff of incense.

On a small table in front of the tent-like canopy stood an old-fashioned oil-lamp housed in a globe of opaque but translucent glass: it shed a circular pool of light around the table, making it like a coloured insert in a monochrome picture. On the table were a large book with a green cover and beside it what looked like a drawing; before it on the floor (she could see its colours now – rich greens, reds and blues) was a plump golden cushion – it seemed to Helen the most natural thing in the world to go and sit on it. The whispering had stopped: she was acutely aware of the silence. The incense smell intensified.

– *Welcome*, a voice said.

It was a most unusual voice, pleasant and melodious, but with a peculiar timbre – it sounded somehow like two voices intertwined. Like the whispering, it seemed to come out of the air, though not from all around – it came from in front of her, and above, as though from someone standing a little way back on the other side of the table.

– *Look at the picture*, said the voice.

It was a sketch on parchment, done in rust-brown ink, executed with great skill: it showed an extraordinary creature, a sort of dragon, bat-winged, with a serpent's tail and the forequarters of an eagle: its curved beak was open, and its head wore a spiked coronet; it stood on top of a slender column, claws clutching the capital.

– *Leonardo da Vinci drew that. It is called "sketch of a fantastic creature" but is actually a drawing of a statue. Such details are important.*

The voice paused to let Helen assimilate this.

– *The book on the table – open it.*

She leaned over the table and opened the book where it lay: it was too heavy to pick up. It was written in a strange script that she guessed was Arabic.

– *The frontispiece.*

Helen turned to it. It was a photograph, of an old-fashioned, grey-hued sort; the background had been blanked out. It showed the same pillar with the same strange creature on top of it.

– *Do you read Turkish?*

– Not in that script, she said, but it seemed to be someone else speaking.

– *The title of the book is* The Secret of the Underground Palace. *It is a rare work, published in Istanbul in the nineteenth century, and suppressed almost immediately. Its author was executed. The Yerebatan Sarayi – the underground palace – is actually a giant cistern, built some fifteen hundred years ago to supply water to the palaces of Byzantium – but the site is much older: it used to be a shrine. The cistern was built to drown the shrine as much as to store water, but people soon forgot that – in fact, for a century or so people forgot even about the cistern itself. Then it was rediscovered, and over the years people began to take more and more interest in it – until the too-inquisitive author of that book went a little too far in his speculations. All entrance to the cistern was forbidden, and when at length it was reopened, over a quarter of it had been bricked up – and remains so to this day.*

Helen gazed at the drawing and the picture side by side, trying to connect them with the events that had led her here.

– What is it? she said at last.

– *What is it?* the voice echoed softly. *What is it indeed?*

It seemed almost to be conferring with itself.

– *It is something that was ancient when those we call the ancients were young. It was old before Moses came out of Egypt. It is the first thing and the last thing: the first and greatest work of hand that our race has ever known; the last surviving – who knows, perhaps the least? – of all the works of some great race that went before us. Perhaps the least!*

From the shadows there came a curious low chuckle.

– *Think of that, Helen* (she noted the use of her name, feeling she ought to be surprised) – *perhaps this marvel that I have sought down the centuries is no more – compared to what* might *have survived – than a pocket watch that, ten thousand years from now, some new primitive will find in a desert that once was Europe. And what will he think then? How will a simple pocket watch that we take for granted – old mechanical technology that we have discarded in favour of quartz crystals and electric batteries – strike the mind of a primitive man? Will he not be awestruck, to find something at once so evidently a work of craft, the work of hands, yet so far beyond anything he could ever make? It will seem to him the handiwork of the gods, a divine thing to be worshipped – to seek to understand it would be wicked, impious – so marvellous a thing could never have any function comprehensible to the mind of mere mortals!*

As he spoke, Helen saw it in her mind – a ragged figure on the sands that buried Florence, Paris, London; glinting in the lean brown fingers the marvellous pocket watch.

When the voice spoke again, it was no longer of an imagined future and a fancied pocket watch but the actual past and an object already unguessably old before the first of the Pharaohs.

– When Byzas came from Megara, to set up the new colony as the oracle at Delphi bade him, it was waiting for him, locked in a pillar of stone. In the midst of their celebrations, lightning struck and the stone crumbled, revealing it. Plato saw it there and marvelled at its reputed great antiquity, saying it was older than Troy; Aristotle saw it too, and remarked that the metal of which it was made showed no sign of age or corrosion. Alexander, Aristotle's pupil, made a special pilgrimage to see it there, and was only with great difficulty dissuaded from taking it away with him. In later times, its secret was lost: ruder hands plucked out its crystal heart – one Licinius, without permission, dismantled its mechanism and made detailed drawings of every part, an impertinence he paid for with his life. It was a foolish act on the part of the authorities, who found they had

no one with the skill to put it back together again. The drawings were long thought to have been destroyed, but they were not; the mechanism was put back, after a fashion, by a bungler whose name has not passed down to us. But long before the iconoclastic wars, when it would surely have been destroyed, the shrine was already drowned and long forgotten in the Yerebatan Sarayi.

As the voice spoke, Helen seemed to see it all, played out in front of her eyes. When it stopped, she sat a while in silence, marvelling. Finally she asked

– Who are you?

– *You already know who I am.*

A different voice spoke, and she had at once the impression of an old man, at once sly and kindly, in a high room in Paris long ago:

– *I thought myself the master, him the pupil*, it said in a rueful tone.

Then another voice said, plaintively

– *I looked with pity on him!*

And with that came the fleeting impression of a young man – little more than a boy – with a long, sensitive face beneath a bonnet of brilliant blue. Then it seemed that one strand of the original double voice untwined, and spoke alone.

– *I know what it is to be young, and set apart by cleverness.*

She saw a young boy studying at a table, poring over books with brilliant eyes.

– *And I know what it is to turn aside from the common way of men.*

She saw on the edge of a grassy dell a grave girl taking her leave of a thin young man: *and so you are going away, Michael – to Paris?* All these things were familiar: where did she know them from? The double voice spoke again

211

– My book speaks only to like minds.

The blue book, of course – she saw it as clearly as if she held it in her hands – but where had it come from? She could not recollect. Moved – drawn? – by a sudden curiosity, she stood up, and went towards the diaphanous canopy. Close to, the incense smell was stronger, but it masked something else she couldn't make out: a sweetish smell. She could see a dark shape inside, humped and massive. Her hand hovered, then she made herself gather a bunch of the material and pull it aside.

She was confronted by a large head on a mountain of silk: someone might have cut it off and laid it there. The head was huge, framed with dark, coarse hair: the skin had a wax-like quality. The eyes were shut. The heavy, full lips were the wrong colour for a living face. The great hook of a nose was fleshy and prominent. It was so grotesque, so like a wax model, that she contemplated it without horror; besides, the face was somehow familiar – it took her some moments to recognize that the features, coarsened by age, were those of the pirate chief in the sea cave, who had bargained with Albanus to free him from captivity.

Then she saw that the lids were trembling slightly. All at once they snapped open, and Helen was aware only of the eyes.

They were the most extraordinary eyes she had ever seen – unusually large, and in that dimness, with widely dilated pupils that gave an impression of immense depth; the irises were almost colourless, like clear water, or diamond. They radiated a powerful sense of will and vitality, in striking contrast to the dead face that housed them – Helen had never had a stronger impression of a spirit existing as something quite separate from the body it inhabited. For a long moment the gaze held her, and she could not look away; then she felt it release her, and the lids fell again.

The face remained a second or two in waxwork immobility, then it was shaken by a tremor: the nostrils twitched, the mouth worked; there was an audible sound of indrawn breath. Helen stepped back, letting the curtain fall, and as she did so, she saw the eyelids open once more, as if from sleep: the eyes they revealed now were dark and baleful, full of malignancy. As she turned and ran, almost sprawling in an effort to avoid the table and the lamp, a horrible stream of words pursued her, a hoarse, wet, bellowing in a language she was glad she could not understand. Even as she reached the door, it came to her that she was safe from pursuit: the angry voice had the same impotent rage as an old man chasing children from his garden. She was more excited than afraid as she fled barefoot down the sloping corridor and along the moonlit passageways.

***

My book speaks only to like minds.
I know what it is to be young, and set apart by cleverness.

Helen sat on her bed in the darkened room, strangely exhilarated, the pantomime horror of the wakening head forgotten: what stayed with her was the power of those diamond eyes, the fascination of that voice, which had reached some place in her that no one else had – giving voice to yearnings she had thought were hers alone:

I know what it is to turn aside from the common way of men

213

Had she not longed to do just that? – to slip out of Helen De Havilland, heiress to a fortune, doomed to a life of dullness by social convention – to discard herself as easily as she had discarded her school uniform from the train: she had a vision of her Aunts gathered in her room at home, gazing bewildered at an empty, crumpled version of herself lying on the bed, like the sloughed skin of a snake.

She saw herself from a completely altered perspective – saw her body as *they* would see it, a mere vehicle, a temporary habitation, like a car you might travel in for a time – her individuality, too, was a mere accident, the product of inhabiting that body at that time in that place – the sensation of freedom was like a breath of cold, fresh air. Everything that she had regarded as most solid, most binding, most inalterable had dissolved into smoke – or rather, what it bound was no longer part of her – she had separated what she thought inseparable, had left her self behind as one might leave a boat securely moored to the bank and slip over the side to swim out to sea...

She had a momentary vision of herself, far out on the boundless ocean, but not alone – up ahead shapes of pure light plunged and soared, flakes of light streaming in trails behind them as they wove in and out, now joined, now separate, a band of liberated spirits, free, immortal, eternal!

She flung herself back on the bed, arms outstretched, in a posture of complete abandonment – she felt as she had once as a little girl (it seemed so long ago) when she had been allowed rather a lot of very fine champagne: her mind was in a pleasant whirl; she felt she could fly up to the ceiling and dance around the room.

She lay a long time with her eyes shut, her senses

withdrawn, lost in a swirling fantasy of a world where everything was possible – she would be like the outermost Russian doll, enclosing Albanus, and Michael Scot, and Michael Scot's ancient Master in Paris – and who knew how many others, or how far back in time the line stretched? The memories she would have access to, the knowledge that would be hers! – like the most amazing private library, stocked with all the wisdom of the ages!

Immersed in her fantasy, she gradually became aware of some persistent, intrusive force: a hand was gripping her ankle, shaking her leg with growing violence.

– Get up! Get up!

The voice was familiar; the setting – a darkened bedroom – and the confusion of her thoughts made her wonder for a moment if she was not back at school, and that everything she had experienced had been some sort of marvellous dream – for there was her room-mate Sophie, quite unmistakable with her strange reddish-woolly hair and skin like soft brown sugar and her different coloured eyes, there was Sophie Petrescu standing at the foot of her bed and shaking her by the ankle. Helen sat up, and tried to clear her head.

– Sophie? Where am I? where did you –

– Get up! You can't stay here! You have to go, hissed Sophie.

– But what – I mean how – what are *you* doing *here*?

Helen demanded, finally managing to assemble the words in the order she wanted.

– I live here.

– You *live* here? But how –

– It is my father's house.

– Your father? Mr. Petrescu?

215

– Petrescu is my mother's name. He calls himself Draganu.

Draganu? A clear light shone into Helen's brain, so bright that she could not see what it revealed.

– You heard what I said. Get up! I do not want you here, supplanting me. I heard what you talked about. First that bitch, getting me into trouble, and now you!

– What are you talking about?

– Put these on.

She thrust a bundle of clothes at Helen.

– I couldn't find your shoes. You'll have to make do with these – they're my sister's.

– I didn't know you had a sister!

– There's a lot you don't know.

– You never mentioned her.

– She's my half-sister.

While she spoke, she was shoving Helen's feet into the borrowed shoes, urging her into the clothes. Suddenly she broke off, seeming unable to contain what she had been brooding on any longer.

– The bitch! She had me wake my father from a trance, phoned me up, all sweet and sugary, told me it would be all right –

A change came over her face: it seemed to crumple and distort. She rocked back, clutching her knees, wailing like a child.

– I didn't mean to, I didn't mean to! She said it would be all right! She said!

Helen, appalled by this sudden collapse, reached out a hand to comfort her. Sophie started as though she had been struck.

– Don't you touch me! You're just the same as her, trying

216

to get me into trouble, trying to supplant me! He hasn't spoken to me for days now because of her, because of what she made me do – he said it could have killed him. I was always his favourite before, now he won't even see me – then he brings you here!

– I didn't ask to be here!

– Good! Well now you can leave. Follow me.

The shock of Sophie's appearance and the urgency of her actions had driven all her recent thoughts from Helen's mind: she was back to the reality of being an abducted schoolgirl again, offered an unexpected chance to escape. She followed Sophie down a narrow corridor – shuffling awkwardly in the too-large shoes – and through a succession of doors, some of which Sophie had to unlock.

– Your half-sister must have big feet, she said to Sophie's back, but received nothing more than an angry gesture to be quiet by way of response.

The house was utterly quiet, and as they stole through the moonlit corridors it was easier for Helen to think that she was in some sort of dream than to believe what was actually happening. They travelled a circuitous route, going up and down many flights of steps, presumably in an effort to avoid the inhabited portions of the house. For all the twists and turns, Sophie never hesitated, and Helen saw with sudden insight that her childhood must have been very like her own, a solitary child finding her own way in rambling, maze-like houses. Watching Sophie's slender back, she felt a surge of sympathy, recalling how they had made friends at once, as soon as they had met; did Sophie feel it too? she wondered. They stole through the darkened house like children playing secret night-time games. At length they came to a small door that took them into the garden, where the sensation of dreamlike unreality persisted: the night air was warm and fragrant – warmer in fact than the house had been – and the huge full moon, making stone walls silver and ivy ink-black against bonewhite marble terraces, gave the whole scene the quality of an etching.

They turned away from the formal gardens down a narrow twisting path that led through a ragged copse, much overgrown – the dew from the wet grass soaked Helen's legs. They emerged into a clearing in front of a high blank wall: ancient gardening tools, long abandoned, leaned against a decaying wheelbarrow, almost submerged in grass. The remains of a neglected, glassless greenhouse huddled in the shadow of the wall.

– You can climb up the greenhouse. The frame is metal, it's stronger than it looks. There's broken glass on the top of the wall but if you put your jacket over it you'll be okay. It's a fair drop on the other side, but it's a soft landing. Follow the road down to the left to get into town.

Helen stood in the moonlight, looking at the almost frail figure of the girl who had once been her friend. She felt a sudden surge of affection for her and leaned forward to embrace her, but Sophie resisted and pushed her away.

– Just go.

They stood a moment longer, Helen looking at the shadowed face, willing some response, some sign of the sympathy and affection she felt must be there, Sophie standing mute, hands hanging by her side. Then Helen turned and scrambled up the frame of the greenhouse, pausing at the top to strip off her jerkin and put it across as Sophie had said; once astride the wall, she looked back down, but there was no one there.

Helen lowered herself until she hung full-length by her arms, then dropped to the ground below: she remembered to keep a grip of her jerkin and brought it down with her, somewhat torn by the broken glass. The road showed grey in the moonlight. She wondered what time it was – two, three in the morning? Then, the ragged jerkin over her arm – the night was too warm to wear it – she shuffled off towards the town in her ill-fitting, borrowed shoes.

The walking cleared her head, and the sense of detachment – an after-effect of whatever they had drugged her with, Helen reckoned – soon wore off, to be replaced by an acute sense of how sore her feet were becoming. She drove herself forward doggedly, welcoming the pain as a kind of penance. She saw now that this was all her fault: if she had not kept a diary, had never confided in Sophie, Stephen Langton might still be alive. The knowledge that Sophie had been sent to spy on her made her betrayal less painful – it was something she had to do, the reason for her being there at all. She could not bring herself to be angry with her. Poor Sophie! She made Helen see her own life in quite a different perspective. What was it she had said about her half-sister, and waking her father from a trance?

In her mind, she connected it with what Raeburn had said about soul-projection, and her father's account of his struggle with Negulescu - *he suddenly seemed to lose all sense of what he was doing: you know, like he had just woken up* – perhaps she had to thank Sophie for that, waking Draganu from his trance and incurring his wrath. And now she had to thank her for her freedom, too – for surely (in spite of all her whirling thoughts earlier) it was better to be here, walking down this road, even with sore feet, than back there, waiting for – what? Some things it was better not to know.

No sooner had the thought occurred than she heard behind her a sound that filled her with dread: a repeated, rhythmic hissing. Without pausing to think, she dived sideways off the road into what she thought was long grass: it turned out to be a ditch. She slithered into the clammy water in a sitting position and found herself peering over the edge of the ditch through clumps of grass. The hissing noise persisted but nothing appeared while Helen sat glumly in the seeping wet. Then all in a moment it swept past, black and enormous, its huge lamps like searchlights sending beams ahead. Helen watched its rear light, like a single red eye, until it was out of sight, and sat for a long time after, despite the discomfort, before she wearily picked her way out of the ditch and stood, dripping, on the road.

With an immense effort of will she put one foot in front of the other and began to walk.

26

The Courtyard of the Basilisk

Following Zoë through the maze of back streets renewed Jake's earlier notion that as they moved away from the main thoroughfare they were plunging deeper into the past: the buildings here seemed very old indeed, with little crooked doorways, and deep window embrasures, mostly shuttered. After many twists and turns through back alleys and little courtyards they came at length to a slit-like entrance between tall buildings, surmounted by an arch. In the weak light Jake saw that the arch itself was carved, but that the work was so ancient that the stone was worn almost smooth again – only a pattern of shadows suggested what might have been a beaked head (which seemed to wear a spiked crown) and a writhing, serpentine body. It had a forbidding look: Jake stood still before it, and Zoë had to reach out to draw him under the arch.

The lane beyond was paved with large flagstones, well worn and cracked in places so that Jake often stumbled in the dim light. As they went on, he found that he held to the centre of the way, troubled by the dark apertures of doors and windows that loomed on either side: it was all too easy to picture surreptitious watchers lurking in the shadows, or worse, to imagine that an arm might come out of the dark and clutch at him. When he looked behind him, the arched entrance seemed very far back. Halfway along, the steps began: the lane plunged abruptly downwards into darkness and the walls closed in on either side: Jake felt for a rail, but his hands met only damp, slippery stone. He was only just aware of the ghostly grey of Zoë's flying suit in front of him, and from time to time the whiteness of her face as she turned to check he was still following.

At length, the steps ended and they were in a low stone corridor – Jake had to stoop to avoid brushing against the roof. He began to imagine that the corridor walls and roof were closing in on him, as he used to dream in childhood nightmares when he would be trapped in an ever-narrowing tunnel until finally there was room only to crawl, and it was impossible to turn around.... how far had they come? The darkness had confused his sense of time, so that he had really no idea if it was only minutes since they had left the café, or if much more time had elapsed. At one point he had a moment of panic when the wall beside him disappeared under his hand, and he stumbled sideways: a stone parapet met him in mid thigh, numbing his leg. He had a sense of openness around him: he guessed they had emerged into a larger space. Far below, he thought he heard the sound of rushing water.

Then the corridor closed in again, and some time after that there were more stairs, climbing this time, in a tight spiral. Up and up they went relentlessly, until Jake felt his legs were like rubber and would carry him no further; but just as he thought so, they emerged into a small moonlit courtyard surrounded by high walls. On the opposite side was a building of primitive simplicity, a plain stone rectangle with two square windows and a central squat doorway: both doorway and windows were deeply recessed, and unpleasantly suggested the features of a face. The stone had a greenish tinge, perhaps from moss or lichen: the whole had an air of unguessable age.

Zoë stooped under the lintel and rapped a complex series of knocks; standing at her back, Jake saw that the lintel stone bore a similar carving to the one on the arched entrance to the lane, a beaked crowned head and a serpentine body.

The door opened, and a tongue of light flicked out across the stone yard. A shadow figure held up an old-fashioned lantern. Zoë and the shadow began a discussion in what Jake supposed was Turkish: he thought he detected a reluctance on the shadow's part to let them in. The voices rose and fell, now harsh, now softer again, until at length Zoë seemed to win the day: the shadow turned and, holding up the lantern, led them inside. From what Jake could see, the interior was filled to the roof on either side with ancient clutter: it was like the storeroom of a shop. They picked their way through the narrow passage that had been preserved amid the towering piles of junk and emerged, stepping down, into a quite different room.

This was cluttered too, but not with junk: everywhere he looked, Jake saw in the mellow golden light the suggestion of some treasure: ornate carved chests of dark wood, inlaid with mother of pearl; marvellous pots, richly enamelled; superb carpets, patterned elaborately in jewel-like colours: red, blue, green and purple; glass vessels encased in filigree brass or silver, with curving stems and mouthpieces, which he guessed were hookahs. Amidst the clutter was a huge mirror, standing on the floor but angled backwards, so that its surface showed no reflection but instead a mysterious rippling subaqueous green like a pool of water.

This is Aladdin's Cave, thought Jake.

Zoë and the shadow man were arguing again: their argument this time seemed to centre on the mirror. The shadow man had set down the lamp to give his hands full play, and he gestured eloquently as he spoke, so that even without understanding the language, Jake could still grasp something of his meaning: he seemed to be invoking some higher authority to refuse Zoë's request; his demeanour suggested that although Zoë outranked him (which was evident from her behaviour) she was asking more than she was entitled to, and that he could not accommodate her without the necessary permission – at several points, he made to leave the room in order to obtain it, but always Zoë drew him back, at first cajoling and entreating, then growing steadily angrier as the shadow man evidently persisted in his stubbornness.

Then she seemed to give up, and change tack, asking now about something to do with the counter behind the man: Jake saw that it seemed a kind of workbench – there was a mortar and pestle on it, and a marble slab with a set of delicate scales; behind was a cabinet, with an array of tiny drawers, all labelled. Zoë seemed to be entreating the man to allow her to mix something – she gestured now at the drawers, now at the mortar, then at herself; but the man angled back his head with a curl of his lip, holding up one hand palm outward while striking the other against his chest, to say that any mixing here would be done by him. They stared at one another in defiance for a time, then Zoë yielded, making submissive gestures and inviting the man to carry on.

He gave a toss of his head and turned to the bench, flicking back his sleeves from his wrists as he considered the array of drawers, his fingers hovering as he homed in on the one to choose – and in one swift, fluid movement, Zoë had crossed the space between them in a stride, clamped her hand over the man's mouth and drawn a broad-bladed knife, which she drove into his back up to the hilt. The man's hands, still held up in front of him, twitched convulsively, then clutched at the edge of the counter as his legs gave way and he slid to the floor.

Jake looked on, paralysed with terror, as Zoë, straddling the body, made a quick survey of the drawers, opened two, then began to dispense their contents onto the scales. She worked with brisk efficiency, emptying the scale into the mortar while with her other hand she searched the drawers again for something else, which she weighed, tipped into the mortar and began to grind. When the preparations were done, she took a pouch from another drawer and carefully transferred the contents of the mortar into it, averting her face to avoid inhaling any of the fine powder. Then she pulled the drawstring tight and turned to Jake, who was still staring at the body.

– Waste no pity on him, she said. He would have shown you none, believe me. We must hurry – Draganu has already taken steps to recover the Thaumatophane.

She took Jake by the shoulders and guided him in the direction of the mirror until they stood in front of it.

– Now, hold this. (she pressed a small glass vial into his hand) I want you to take a deep breath and hold it until I finish doing this.

She undid the drawstring of the pouch and carefully emptied some of the powder into the vial: a fine plume of dust went up from it like smoke. The pouring seemed to take an age: Jake could feel his heart pumping. At last she put the stopper in and Jake let out a grateful stream of breath – but just as he drew in on the reflex, Zoë twitched her hand slightly and sent a cloud of powder from the pouch in her hand up in front of his face, where he had no choice but to inhale it deeply.

Several things seemed to happen at once, and Jake saw them in a strange, fragmented way, like reflections in the facets of a diamond: in front of him, he saw the mirror swing slowly upright; he was aware of Zoë behind him, transferring her hands from his shoulders to his head, so that her fingertips pressed his temples; to one side, his eye was distracted by the absurd fact that a big ornamental clock on a sideboard had chosen this very moment to go haywire: its hands suddenly began sweeping round its face at a ridiculous speed. In his head, the thought *she's tricked me* seemed to hang in mid air; at the same time, he had a sense of Zoë as a predatory presence, invading his mind, and he was seized with a desperate urge to evade her – he saw himself as a tiny mouse, darting behind a curtain to escape a searching cat – *if I can just curl up here and be still*, he thought, *she might not notice me.*

In front of him, the mirror was fully upright, and for a moment he saw himself, mouth open in a perfect O of astonishment, with Zoë standing behind him, hands to his temples, like a priestess – then the surface of the mirror seemed to dissolve into a blackness as deep as the cosmos.

In his head, Jake saw himself again as the mouse, now creeping out from behind the curtain – he sensed that the cat-like danger of Zoë was still very close, but at the same time directed elsewhere...he crept forward.

He saw a figure in a darkened room, moving stealthily. *That is me*, he thought with astonishment. The tiny particle of his mind that remained his own told him, *this is something you are seeing in the mirror.* The figure moved methodically about the room, searching for something. It seemed to be a hotel room: there was a large bed, which had not been slept in, and a suitcase on the floor beside it. On a table, there was a map, and a piece of paper with directions: next to it was a battered red metal box. Jake saw all this over the figure's shoulder, yet at the same time he was quite certain that the figure was himself. *This must be some kind of rehearsal,* he thought, *to show me what I am to do.* He also felt sure that he was not supposed to be witnessing it, and the thought gave him some kind of hope. *She's programming me,* he thought, *but she doesn't realise that I am still conscious.*

The figure had opened the box now, and there in a nest of black velvet lay the crystal. Swiftly, the figure drew out an identical crystal and substituted it, slipping the original into a pocket, and then closed the box again. Just at that moment, the figure started, as at an unexpected sound: it moved stealthily towards the communicating door, just as it opened, and Helen stepped into the room.

Jake felt a shock of anguished delight at seeing her: she wore a white night-dress, and seemed barely awake; she rubbed a hand across her eyes. The figure by the door uncorked a vial and, emptying some of its contents onto its palm, blew them lightly into Helen's face as she turned, a look of wonder on her face – she seemed on the verge of speaking, then her eyes rolled in her head, and she meekly allowed herself to be guided back to her room. Jake in his head was conscious of making a great effort of will, and as he did, his viewpoint seemed to change, so that he was no longer behind the figure, but actually one with it: he could feel the softness of Helen's shoulders through the thin material as he walked her across the room.

When they reached her bed, he drew back the cover, and when he exerted a small pressure on her elbow, she obediently climbed in, like a sleepwalking child – she had an odd sort of dazed expression on her face: a faintly puzzled smile played about her lips. All this time, Jake was in a kind of agony of delight – it was the paradox of being awake in a beautiful dream, so that you are aware of it in every wonderful detail, yet aware at the same time that it is only a dream – in a kind of despair, he reached out to Helen, hoping to wake her up, and in that instant, he sensed that Zoë had detected him – he lost control of his arm, and it flailed down onto the bedside table, clutching at something and gathering it up – one of Helen's earrings.

Then all at once he was outside himself again, seeing the figure stagger to its knees, then scramble up again: but the whole scene seemed to fade, the colours merging into greyness that deepened into black – then, with a start, he was fully awake, and staring at his own reflection in the mirror.

27
Meeting Mr. Dormouse

Helen woke to the sun streaming into her room and the now almost familiar sensation of having no idea where she was; she felt very relaxed, as after a profound sleep. Gradually recollection returned: she was in Turkey, in a hotel overlooking the Black Sea; and she had been having a most extraordinary dream – Sophie had been in it, and a black car – she had been walking, and her feet hurt – which they still did. She swung her legs over the side of the bed and examined her feet: they were indeed raw and blistered in several places. So it had not been a dream, then: the other details came back to her. She had been kidnapped, had escaped, narrowly avoided recapture and had returned to the hotel, exhausted and footsore, surprised to find it was not long after midnight. Fortunately she had her keycard with her. Her father had not been there: she wondered if he was now.

She padded gingerly to the connecting door and

knocked lightly: no reply. She went in. The room was empty;
the bed had not been slept in – or it might have been made
up. What time was it? she could not find her watch. On the
table was a scatter of things she remembered from the
evening before, among them a street map and a card bearing
the name and address of Michael Palaeologlu: that was the
collector who was buying the Machine – a friend of Stephen
Langton's, she supposed. Her father had gone to see him:
perhaps he had spent the night there. Helen laughed: was it
possible that her whole incredible adventure had passed
entirely unremarked? It seemed that it might have. That
increased the quality of unreality which clung about the
whole thing. It was an effort to believe that she had been
abducted from the street outside: might she not be in danger
still?

She crossed to the window and surveyed the street: no
sinister black cars were parked alongside the pavement; there
were no idlers or knots of suspect people; only a few very
obvious tourists strolled in couples, and a street sweeper
pushed a dustbin mounted on bicycle wheels. Cars passed
up and down. Beyond the road, the Black Sea glittered in
the strong sunshine; there was a haze further out, and in it
she could see the outline of several large ships going to and
fro. It was difficult to associate the scene with the fantastic
occurrences of the night, and difficult to convince herself
that she was still in any immediate danger – she felt
deliciously lazy and at ease. Apart from my feet, she thought,
shifting to relieve the ache. A hot bath is in order, then I can
think what to do next.

She emerged three-quarters of an hour later shrouded
in steam, her feet greatly soothed, and ravenously hungry.

She ordered breakfast and considered her next step. If her father had not appeared by the time she had eaten, she would leave a note and go to Mr. Palaeologlu's. She would remain alert, keeping an eye out for any possible danger, even though she did not believe she would encounter any in the short journey along the waterfront.

She ate her breakfast and dressed in a leisurely manner, glad to have brought a pair of sandals so minimal in construction that they could not possibly chafe her feet. At the hotel entrance, she made herself look carefully up and down the street and scrutinize everyone in the vicinity: she felt faintly ridiculous, like a child playing at being a secret agent. When she had satisfied herself that there was nothing that looked even remotely threatening, she crossed the road and strolled along the sunlit pavement, looking out across the dazzling sea.

What a fascinating part of the world this was: people had lived here for time out of mind. Its history stretched back through a succession of empires into myth and legend: before the Ottomans, the Eastern Roman Empire had survived nearly a thousand years beyond the fall of Rome: there had been no Dark Ages here. The Greeks and the Persians had fought over this territory: Cyrus the Great had chastised the sea for wrecking the bridge of boats he built across the Hellespont. Just a little way to the south, on the opposite shore, her namesake Helen had brought war on Troy; through the very waters she was looking at now, Jason and the Argonauts had sailed, in search of the Golden Fleece.

She found herself wishing strongly that Jake was there to share it with – but which one, she asked herself? The Jake she had in mind was the carefree boy whose company she had shared in Florence, cheerful, unselfconscious Jake who had been fun to be with. That was less than a year ago, she reminded herself. Why could it not be like that again? Why did there have to be all this angst and moodiness, the languishing sighs, the droopy looks? Why can't we spare that till later, if we have to have it at all, and just have a good time? Thinking of Jake sparked the recollection that she had dreamed about him last night – but try as she might, the details of it would not come to her.

Looking up, she saw that her musing had brought her to Mr. Palaeologlu's house, an elegant white villa on the shore with door and shutters painted a striking shade of blue: it looked to be built out over the water. While she was contemplating the door, it opened and a little old man came out. He was fastidiously neat, with white hair, a neatly-trimmed beard, and very dark eyes; his fingers were long and elegant, his feet tiny, encased in shiny patent leather. He gave her a pleasant, inquisitive smile. He reminded Helen of a dormouse.

– You are looking for my nephew, I think – I am, alas! past that age when beautiful young ladies call upon me.

– Are you Mr. Palaeologlu?

– I am indeed, but then so is he.

– The friend of Stephen Langton?

– I fail you again, I fear – I seem to know the name, but I could not claim acquaintance.

– Then I'm afraid it must be your nephew I want, smiled Helen.

– Alas! His gain, my loss. What name shall I say?

– De Havilland: Helen De Havilland.

The little man could not have become more animated if he had suddenly touched a bare electric wire.

– Impossible! Impossible! he exclaimed. It cannot be! You are never *Gerry's* daughter? He gave me the impression you were just a child! Let me look at you! Such a splendid young woman! You are most welcome!

And to Helen's surprise he embraced her joyfully, kissing her on either cheek.

– Come in, come in! he urged. I hardly expected you this early!

Helen followed him into the cool interior, considerably puzzled at the warmth of her reception. Her father must have made a considerable impression last night to cause such an effusive reaction.

– Your father is not with you, I take it? I did not think he would return so soon.

– No, said Helen, I'm on my own.

– But it is so good to see you! And as I say, such a surprise! Let me look at you!

But of course, she thought, it's getting the Alchemist's Machine he's pleased about – that's what makes him so well disposed to the De Havillands. Collectors, she knew, regarded their acquisitions with more affection than some people accorded their children.

– On such an auspicious day, it can hardly be too early for a drink!

He busied himself with something at the sideboard, then presented Helen with a tall glass of clear liquid, tinkling with ice cubes. She sipped it cautiously. How old does he think I am? she wondered.

– Let us go out on the terrace.

Helen followed him through tall shuttered doors onto a fine veranda that ran the length of the house. It looked across to the entrance to the Bosphorus. Insubstantial in the haze, great ships passed up and down. Near at hand, the white sails of dinghies tacked back and forth.

– What a beautiful view!

– Is it not? said Mr. Palaeologlu. He gave a contented sigh.

For a time they just stood gazing out across the waters, side by side, arms resting on the veranda rail. At length Mr. Palaeologlu observed,

– Your father, my dear, is in his own way something of a great man. It would not be going too far to say that he is an artist in his field.

Well that's a bit over the top, thought Helen. Still, I suppose he's entitled to be pleased with his new acquisition: if that makes him think better of Dad, well and good. She was watching, with one eye shut against the glare, the progress of a yacht that seemed intent on crossing the mouth of the Bosphorus, rather like an intrepid pedestrian making a dash across a busy road. The reflected light made it appear to be sailing on a sea of molten gold.

– I tell him that he should write a book, the story of all the deals he has made.

Dad's obviously been spinning his yarns again, thought Helen. The yacht was now on a collision course with a small coaster. Who will give way? She wondered. Sail before steam – isn't that the rule? But then cars are supposed to give way to pedestrians too.

– And now is the time to do it, you know.

The yacht shot across the bows of the coaster: I bet there's some hard swearing going on out there, she thought. She became aware that Mr. Palaeologlu was asking her a question.

- After all, he is hardly likely to surpass this latest exchange, is he?

The little man beamed and rubbed his hands. Helen, having taken her eyes off the yacht to attend to the question, tried to locate it again. Ah, there it was! After its triumph over the coaster, the yacht now seemed intent on ramming a huge tanker, running so light that it seemed to sit on top of the water, like a child's drawing of a ship.

- Hitherto, mere money has been his object – but this, now – an altogether nobler thing, do you not think?

I really haven't the faintest what he's on about, but I don't care, she thought, so long as I can stand here and gaze at the view. Why is that? I suppose because the Machine is no longer our problem – it's passed to Mr. Palaeologlu. It's his door Draganu will come to next. She felt a pang of guilt, looking at the little man: does he know what he's let himself in for? The yacht had tacked, and now appeared to be racing the tanker, its white sails vivid against the dull red of its lower hull.

- So I said to him, "Gerry, if you can pull this off, you should think of retiring."

Out at sea, the yacht was gaining on its giant opponent. He surely can't mean to cut across his bows the way he did the coaster? thought Helen. They won't be able to see him so close up.

- And, if I may speak confidentially, my dear, you should encourage him. A man has only so much luck in a lifetime – your father has already used more than most.

Something in the way he said it caught Helen's attention: he might almost have made a study of Dad's career, she thought. She began to wonder if perhaps she had misinterpreted Mr. Palaeologlu's position.

– Mr. Palaeologlu, how long have you known my father, exactly?

– Exactly? It is difficult to say, it has been such a long time.... since we were both much younger, certainly.

He smiled at some recollection of his youth. Comprehension was dawning rapidly on Helen.

– So you are one of the "old crowd?"

– Perhaps the oldest! he began, with pride. Then, catching the note of disapproval, the old man wagged a reproving finger at her. Now, now, Miss! You must not be so high and mighty – who else could have put him in touch with Draganu at such short notice?

– Draganu !?

Now it was Palaeologlu's turn to look puzzled.

– Of course, Draganu!

– *You* were acting as a middleman for *Draganu*?

He seemed quite at a loss to comprehend Helen's expression of horror.

– Well, that was the intention of course – though in the event, given the turn things took last night, your father preferred to deal with him directly, and give him the Machine in person –

– He *gave* it to *Draganu*?

– But of course... as a ransom for you –

28
The Underground Palace

Under other circumstances, Helen would probably have found the speed-boat ride exhilarating: it had just that element of danger she needed to remind her she was alive. Young Mr. Palaeologlu – the nephew – seemed utterly fearless, or perhaps just crazy, but there was no doubt that he was in his element, swerving and leaping his way down the narrow channel, diving through openings impossibly small, earning a varied chorus of warning blasts from startled vessels. Soon the buildings of Istanbul reared up on either side: amazing waterside villas with ornate filigree balconies on every level, and huge arched caverns at water level as ordinary houses might have basement garages. When they veered in close to shore, Helen could see the roads were choked with traffic. Let Dad be caught in it, she implored, let him break down. She tried to visualize a stalled taxi, gushing clouds of steam: perhaps if she imagined it vividly enough, it might happen. Just let me arrive ahead of him, please.

They swept under the majestic line of the Bosphorus Bridge – joining two continents – and set a course direct for Seraglio Point: from the map, Helen could see two roads running up through Gulhane Park almost direct to the Yerebatan Sarayi. She tried to pick them out from the green slope ahead: they must run up to the right of the complex and impressive clutter of the Topkapi Sarayi. At the top of the hill was the fantastic outline of Hagia Sophia, a giant beehive hedged about with spears.

– Thanks for the trip, said Helen, it was very kind of you.

Mr. Palaeologlu's nephew gave a good-natured flap of the hand, indicating that the pleasure had been his, and brought the boat alongside with impressive accuracy. Helen sprang ashore and started to run.

She raced up the steps to the street above, ran along that and came to a busy road, beyond which she could see an entrance to the park. Fortunately, the traffic had slowed almost to a standstill, so she dashed across, dodging in and out of the slow-moving throng of cars. Once in the park she toiled upwards through the masses of tourists going to and from the Topkapi Palace. It was strange to be hurrying past a place which a short time before she had been thinking of as one she must visit with Jake. How easy it would be to turn aside, to join in with the rest and become just another sightseer! She wondered how many of the tourists that she hurried past were suffering that feeling of vague discontent that visits you when, in a place where romantic and exciting things have happened, you wish something of the kind would happen to you – yet here she was, hurrying to adventure, wishing she could turn aside.

She arrived, panting, at the top of the slope and found an exit that took her onto a large plaza. The huge bulk of Hagia Sophia reared up to the left, some way ahead; she knew that the entrance to the Yerebatan Sarayi lay just opposite, at one end of the Hippodrome. She hurried along the crowded pavement and the Blue Mosque came into view, rising from the trees, like Hagia Sophia's younger and more beautiful sister. Then across the road she saw something which stopped her dead in her tracks, as if a character from a nightmare had walked into the open day: the black car, huge and sinister. It was parked beside a low blockhouse of a building which looked like nothing so much as a public convenience, but as soon as she saw it, Helen guessed that this must be the entrance to the Yerebatan Sarayi.

She hurried across and was fortunate enough to be able to attach herself to a party of tourists who were just going in: she followed them down the steep staircase and into the chamber below. It was vast. In the dimness, rows of pillars like petrified trees marched away on every side: the eerie lighting, reflected from the water that covered the floor, cast strange rippling reflections on the vaulted brickwork high overhead. Music played, lent a weird, unearthly quality by the peculiar acoustic. The tourist party, awed into silence, shuffled along the echoing wooden walkway that ran in and out of the labyrinth of pillars. The voice of the guide discoursing on the wonders of the place came back to Helen, distorted to unintelligibility by a ringing echo. Deeper and deeper they went until they came to something that might once have been a fountain. The pillars here had Gorgons' heads at the base, stained green with water and rendered still more grotesque by being upside-down.

Further on they came to another walkway branching off at right angles: its entrance was closed with a chain on which hung a sign in several languages forbidding entry. The walkway zigzagged among the pillars, almost lost in the dimness: the lights in that section had been switched off. Helen unhooked the chain and slipped quietly along the walkway. The voice of the guide grew more distant: she was aware of the drip of water from above, a melancholy sound. She saw that the walkway ended abruptly in the middle of the water; but as she drew nearer, she was able to make out some sort of pulley arrangement that ran into the darkness. Peering ahead, she thought she could just make out what might have been the outline of a boat: it was moored up against a brick wall that did not seem in keeping with the rest of the stonework. With a thrill, she remembered what Michael Scot had said: that a quarter of the chamber had been bricked up in the nineteenth century, following the suppression of the book, *The Secret of the Underground Palace*. This had to be the place.

She hauled on the rope. The pulley squealed as the slack took up, then the rope went taut. Helen pulled harder, and all at once whatever was at the other end freed itself with a splash. She saw the boat coming towards her through the dimness; did she also see something moving on the far side by the wall, where the boat had been? It was impossible to tell: perhaps it was just the shadow of the boat. When the boat came up, she saw it was more a raft or floating platform, attached to the pulley by a rope from either end. She clambered aboard and quickly began to pull herself across, fearful that the squealing pulley would attract attention; but the tourist party seemed to have moved to some distant part of the cistern, out of earshot. The raft ground against an underwater ledge and Helen stepped out into a thin layer of cold water.

At the foot of the brick wall she saw that there was a square alcove, sufficiently wide and deep for a man to stand in. She stepped into it. To her right, her hand encountered rough brick; to her left, empty space. She turned towards it, took a deep breath and then went in; her outstretched hand again found brick. Swivelling cautiously round, she found that the passage turned at right angles. She groped her way forward a few paces and the wall to her right disappeared from under her hand; looking there, she saw a perceptible lightening of the darkness and could just make out the dim outline of a doorway not far ahead. She made her way cautiously towards it. On the threshold, she saw the reason for the dimness: the space in front of the opening was a maze of columns, with whatever light there was filtering through it from beyond. After studying it for a time, Helen saw that there were three rows of pillars, curving away on either side; the maze effect was created by the middle row, which was out of alignment with the other two, so that the only way through was by a zigzag route. She advanced to the column directly in front of her, moved stealthily round it, then darted across to the rear of the next ahead: she was now behind the inmost row. Which side should she look out?

As she was pondering, a voice said,

– You can come out now. I know you're there.

Helen felt a strange tingle in her stomach that was only partly dread: the voice was the same as that she had heard the night before, the twin interwoven voices of Michael Scot and Albanus. She stepped out from behind the column: was it a trick of the light, her own shadow perhaps, or did she see out of the corner of her eye another figure draw back, as though it too had been about to obey the summons of the voice, but had changed its mind?

The space she stood on the edge of was almost spherical: the colonnade ran round its circumference, with a domed roof overhead; at her feet, the floor fell steeply away to form a wide bowl. From its centre a circular pedestal, composed of concentric tiers of stone, supported a slender column, topped with a statue that she recognized at once: the Bronze Basilisk. Around the base of the pedestal three huge tripods supported shallow basins filled with blazing oil; beside one of these, two standing figures flanked a massive shape in an outsize wheelchair. Helen wondered how they had managed to manoeuvre it through the colonnade and down the concave slope.

– Helen!

The voice spoke, as before, out of the air, at some height above the ground. Did she imagine it, or was there an intonation of surprise there, as if someone else had been expected to step forward?

– Come down.

Helen eased herself down onto the curving floor, slithering a little way until she found her footing. Walking carefully down towards the centre, she had the most extraordinary sensation of being in two places at once: without losing sight of her surroundings, she was somehow aware of being on the slope of a grassy dell, out of doors; overhead, clouds raced across a blue sky driven by a great wind in the heavens. Standing in front of her was a dark young man, remarkably thin, with a radiance in his face that made him immensely attractive. She heard herself say – in a strange, thick accent she could barely make out – *So, Michael, you are going away? To Paris?* – but she knew the words had been uttered only in the dell, not here in the chamber. The young man did not reply, but looking in his face, at those bright, bright eyes, she saw the answer there. *He will not come back: he is lost to me.* The thought filled her with a huge, aching sorrow.

Then a sudden, awful yell shredded the fabric of her dream and she saw in horror the bulky figure in the chair rise up and stumble towards her, raging and spitting: its arms lashed out, fingers clawing the air. Helen was rooted to the spot in terror. The figure halted, swaying, after a few steps; then all at once it crumpled, like a puppet with its strings cut, and the attendants hurrying up behind caught it in the chair, where it slumped, inert. After a moment's silence the voice spoke again, but the idyll of the green dell did not return; instead the voice had an edge to it, an insinuating, sarcastic tone:

– You must forgive Mr. Draganu these outbursts. He was ever a man of uncertain temper, even in health, and now that he feels the approach of death and the added insult of betrayal –

– Betrayal? said Helen.

She felt a sinking fear.

– By his daughter.

Helen blenched. She felt she had walked into a trap.

– He trusted her, you see, as a father does his daughter. He planned to give her everything, but she did not want to be his heir –

The voice spoke coldly, and not just to Helen, but for the world to hear, inviting witness to what it said. Helen stood rigid, staring ahead of her, seeking some distraction from her fear: between the pillars above and behind Draganu's chair was an odd pattern of light and shadow that drew her eye, perhaps because it vaguely suggested a human figure. She concentrated her gaze on it, trying to resolve it into its separate elements. That bit, now, was like an arm, but only because the paler patch at the end suggested a hand; and that other light bit was like one side of a face cut in two by shadow, but only because it was at the right height; and there was really nothing else to it – the rest was just darkness. Then either the light shifted subtly, or Helen's eyes adjusted in some way, and she saw that it actually was a figure. She felt her eyes widening and tried to stop them for fear it would betray what she had seen. It was Sophie. How had she got there? He knows she is there, she thought, that is why he is talking like this. It is meant for her as much as me. The voice continued relentlessly, now chillingly light in its tone:

– But even the most loving fathers do not tell their daughters everything – as I think you know yourself – and there is always more than one way to gain what you seek.

Helen looked at Sophie, tense and still between the pillars. She tried to will her to get away, to hide herself.

– And every experience teaches something, as they say, and this fondness of fathers for their daughters can be turned to good account, as I found last night.

Here there was a whispering sound that might have been laughter.

– Your own father was only too willing – you will be glad to hear – to exchange the Thaumatophane for you, though I do believe he had hoped to make profit of a more material kind. But he can hardly think himself hard done by, to give what is rightfully mine for what is rightfully his.

Helen saw that the air above the figure in the wheelchair was disturbed in some way: it rippled like waves of heat, and something danced and scintillated there, a host of tiny diamond-bright sparks of light that came and went unceasingly. Whatever it was lay between her and Sophie, so that Helen could no longer make her out.

– And now your father comes once more to redeem you, bringing the crystal heart of the Bronze Basilisk – it is a precious treasure, but scarcely too great a price to pay for such a one.

The tone now was almost playful: my god, thought Helen, he's *flirting* with me – yet all the time, she felt the conversation was actually meant for someone else.

– Think now: the Stone was given as a dowry once – might it not be so again? What do you say? Would you accept the legacy another spurns?

Helen felt her heart turn over: the dancing glitter in the bending air held her – how beautiful, how *vital* it was! All the surrounding space had darkened, or slipped behind a veil: there was only herself and this dancing spirit, inviting her – she opened her mouth to speak.

– Helen – are you all right?

Startled back to reality, she saw her father emerge from the colonnade: he hurried down the slope to embrace her, clutching something in his hand.

– Ah, the crystal! said the voice in the air. Perhaps if you were to bestow it on your daughter, she could perform the final office?

Helen's father looked at her anxiously: she nodded to reassure him, and held out her hand. Reluctantly, he dropped the crystal into it.

Turning, she began to ascend the pedestal.

– Wait! said a voice.

29
The Moment of Truth

It took Jake a moment to realise where he was: oddly, the first thing he noticed was the sonorous tick of the clock, which seemed to have resumed its normal behaviour. The next thing he registered was that he was alone: Zoë was no longer behind him. He turned full circle, peering into the gloom. There was no sign of her. By the counter, the body still lay sprawled on the floor, and the sight of it chilled him: he remembered the swift, sudden movement as Zoë had come up behind him with the knife, the ruthless and efficient slaughter that followed. Whoever she was, and whatever she was up to, he wanted no part of it: his one desire was to get as far away from here as possible.

He stood a moment, considering: the route he had followed in was long and tortuous, and it took a long time to reach anywhere – there were rather too many dark stairs and tunnels between him and any possibility of escape; the idea of being pursued through them did not bear thinking about – nor did the feeling that there had been lurking watchers as they passed – watchers, he felt sure, who had only been deterred by Zoë's presence. There must surely be some other way out, he thought, moving cautiously into the darkness beyond the mirror, where there seemed to be a path picked out among the shadowy accumulations of stuff.

The path led to a curtain, which he pulled aside to reveal a door. Carefully, he tried the handle: it opened onto blackness. He hesitated, then stepped inside. The door swung shut behind him, and he was assailed by panic – it was utterly dark. Then the floor fell away beneath him, and it was all he could do to stifle a scream. Fortunately the drop did not last – he had just time to register that he must be in some sort of lift, when it eased to a gentle halt. Fumbling in front of him, he found a handle: the door opened inwards, to reveal a curtain with light shining beyond it. He took a deep breath, and pulled it aside.

He was in a stone chamber, entirely bare, and of moderate size: there were curtained entrances in each wall. Standing by one of them was Zoë. She had changed out of her flying suit, and now wore a simple white robe, caught at the waist with a belt of gold rings; the heavy bracelets on her bare arms gave her the look of a pagan goddess. There was something beside her on the floor, covered with a dark red cloth. Jake stared at her a moment, then turned back to the door and made to go through it –

He found himself teetering on the brink of a dark shaft, clutching at the doorjamb with one hand, while the other tried desperately to keep the door from swinging any further away from him.

– Counterweights, said Zoë matter-of-factly. The lift

goes back up as soon as you step out of it.

Jake levered himself back into the room and stood panting.

– We have to go now, said Zoë. Timing is critical.

She pulled at something behind the curtain and after a moment or two the whole chamber began to slink slowly into the ground. Jake could only gape.

– Counterweights? he croaked at last.

Zoë smiled and nodded.

– Built fifteen centuries ago, and still working perfectly – a remarkable piece of engineering.

She spoke calmly, but she radiated excitement like an electric field. Jake felt stunned – awed by her presence, and completely unable to think of what to do to save himself. The room settled with a click.

Zoë gathered up the bundle from the floor, drew the curtain aside and ushered Jake through: a vaulted passageway led to a larger opening between tall columns. She steered him along the passage with a hand on the back of his neck, then stopped while they were still some way short of the end. She passed a hand over his face and he felt all his muscles become lethargic and heavy: he was powerless to move or speak. Zoë stole forward and waited in the shadow of the entrance, listening intently. Jake heard voices coming from somewhere beyond, but could not make out what they were saying. He had no idea how long he had stood before Zoe's imperious gesture stirred him back to life and summoned him to her side. She placed her hand on his neck once more, and together they stepped out into the space beyond.

– Wait! said Zoe in a commanding tone.

Helen, at the foot the pedestal, the crystal in her hand, turned to see a tall figure clad in white standing in the gap in the colonnade: in her right hand, she carried something veiled with a red cloth; at her side was Jake. It took Helen a moment to recognize where she had seen the face before: in London, in her father's flat.

Zoë moved down the steps, pushing Jake ahead of her. All eyes were on her: over Draganu's head, the shimmering in the air disappeared – the massive bulk in the wheelchair stirred, and began to rise. Zoë halted halfway, Jake on the step below her, and waited until Draganu stood upright, swaying slightly, staring at her, his right arm extended towards her in accusation. Then she spoke:

– Father!

Father? Helen's eyes darted from Draganu to Zoë and back again, seeking some resemblance. *She is Sophie's half sister*, she thought. Draganu stood swaying like a drunkard: his mouth worked, struggling to frame words. With a flourish, Zoë drew aside the red cloth:

– I come to do your will!

In her right hand was a silver basin; in her left, a long curved blade.

– See – I bring the instruments of sacrifice! I come to claim my inheritance!

Helen saw the colour drain from Jake's face. Zoë held up a forbidding hand to Helen, and gestured to her father.

– *You* should insert the crystal: it is only fitting."

Draganu seemed to consider this, then swung ponderously towards Helen, taking clumsy, stiff-legged steps, his hand held out in front of him.

– Give it to me, he said hoarsely.

Close to, he was a giant of a man: though Helen was

standing a step up the pedestal, he still towered over her. She dropped the crystal in his outstretched hand: his fingers closed about it, greedily. She stepped back, but not soon enough to avoid his hand which pressed down on her shoulder with crushing weight as he thrust himself upwards onto the first step. Helen backed away as soon as he lifted his hand from her. It was agonizing to watch his laboured progress as he hauled himself step by step up the pedestal. When he was close enough, he stretched out a long arm, seizing the slender pillar that supported the statue, and levered himself up. He stood, swaying, over the statue, steadying his hand above the open hatchway in its back, a look of malignant triumph on his face; then slowly – almost gently – he put the crystal in place, and closed the door over it. He gave one final look around the chamber, and pressed the switch forward.

There was a dull click, clearly audible in the tense silence.

Nothing happened.

Jake, staring white faced, saw Zoë turn towards him, with a disconcerting smile. She *winked*. Jake's fingers, fumbling nervously in his pocket, felt something there and drew it out. It was Helen's earring. With dawning comprehension, he looked at Zoë – her eyes now were fixed on Draganu, an expression of triumphant malice on her face: she had set the basin aside, and was reaching for something in the folds of her dress.

Draganu stood gaping at the impotent Basilisk, wearing a look of shock and utter disbelief: then, uttering a stream of guttural oaths, he seized it with both hands, trying to wrench it from the pillar – but the effort overbalanced him: he flung one arm out behind in an effort to recover and for a moment he hung there, supported only by his grip on the statue – then his own massive weight prised his fingers from their hold and he toppled headlong with a despairing cry, slithering and scrabbling down the steps to end in a huge crumpled heap at the foot. The two attendants started forward, but stopped in their tracks when Zoë swung her arm up in an imperious gesture: her hand glowed red from the light concealed within it; at the same time, a wave of resonant sound swept across the chamber, so deep that it was felt rather than heard.

She opened her fingers and revealed a pulsing light: the thaumatophanic crystal.

She held it out towards the prostrate Draganu in mockery, as he writhed on the floor, clutching impotently with his outstretched hand. The waves of sound pulsed through the chamber, increasing in intensity.

It was like a tableau: Zoë, the pulsing crystal held aloft; Draganu sprawled at her feet; the others looking on – then Sophie Petrescu came bounding down the steps and launched herself onto her half-sister's back like a wild animal.

Zoë, sent flying, cannoned into Jake; the crystal, flung from her hand, seemed to hang in the air, then dropped towards Draganu – but Jake, stumbling forward, reached out and caught it as neatly as a cricket-ball.

It's cold, he thought. I expected it to burn.

He gazed at his hand, pulsing redly, then slowly opened his fingers. The crystal sparked and vibrated like a living thing: he stared at it, fascinated.

– Jake! Look out! shouted Helen.

He turned to look at her and at the same time felt a heavy impact against his legs as Draganu heaved himself forward in a last despairing effort to seize the Stone. Jake twisted and fell, Draganu's arms scrabbling at him, pulling him off balance.

– To me! cried Helen.

Jake was rolling as he fell, entangled with Draganu's bulk, but he managed to get a clear swing with his arm and sent the crystal spinning upwards in the vibrant air. The throw seemed to be coming to Helen, but as she watched, the Stone appeared to swing in flight and bend towards the Basilisk. Her eyes fixed on it, she sprang up the steps, feeling the statue shake as she grabbed at it for support – then she held her arm aloft, and the stone flew to her hand like a bird.

As soon as she held it, Helen felt a surge of energy course down her arm and through her body, into the statue under her hand: the panel on its back sprang open, and the false crystal was ejected like a flung stone, falling to shatter in pieces on the steps. Her vision was transformed: the solid building around her was drawn in lines of light; she could see beyond it, not merely into space, but time: it was as if her mind had expanded to contain the universe, as if the whole of creation from its very beginning was present to her simultaneously. Within the chamber she saw, not people, but forms of moving light – her eyes could penetrate material things and see beyond them to the life itself: that must be her father; that was Jake; those two, intertwined, were Sophie and the woman – all of them were where their bodies had been, and indeed she could faintly see their bodies too, like some transparent envelope; the exception was Draganu, who seemed a black, dead bulk – but above it hovered the most brilliant spirit of them all, a shimmering constellation of diamond points of light, dancing in the air.

All seemed to wait on her.

She held the Stone aloft like a trophy, feeling the energy pulse down her arm, flowing through her and into the slender metal pillar that supported the statue; the bell-like sound was now an insistent throb that filled the chamber. The thought came clearly to her mind: *put it in the statue.* Looking down, she saw the Bronze Basilisk and its inner mechanism etched in lines of sapphire light, all in tremendous detail, as through a magnifying glass: it seemed super-real. She could see each tiny scale on the body, each delicate component of the mechanism within; she saw below a loop of chain and a curiously slender pin that secured the statue to the top of the pillar. *Do it now,* came the thought again, more insistent this time. The diamonds in the air kindled to an intense brightness; the stone became massively heavy: the statue seemed to draw it down.

With a sense almost of performing a sacrament, Helen lowered her arm and placed the Stone in the waiting recess. The bell-like humming ceased and something like a sigh seemed to run through the air all round her; the pulsing of the stone settled to a steady brilliance. Helen's vision returned to normal; she felt her mind empty of everything save the awesome simplicity of her task: *I am a handmaid,* she mused. Her fingers caressed the outside of the bronze panel lightly, feeling the texture of the scales – *this, now, is the last moment that I might turn aside,* she thought – *this is my Garden of Eden moment, when the fruit of the tree is offered to me. What shall I do?*

Gently, almost tenderly, she pressed it shut.
It closed with a tiny click.
She pushed the little lever forwards.
At once the room was rocked by an enormous jolt like an earthquake, accompanied by a gigantic noise like a thunderclap. From inside the statue a whirring hum began, as of something rotating with ever-increasing speed, and

from the basilisk's open beak a thin blade of intensely bright light shot out and struck the opposite wall. As the beam of light widened and thickened, the wall of the chamber where it shone seemed to dissolve; the humming rose in pitch and intensity. Helen, her hands still on the statue, felt it vibrate with barely-contained energy; watching the growing patch of light she felt overcome with awe. *What have I done?* she asked herself. She felt on the verge of revelation: something is about to happen, she thought, something wonderful and terrible.

Now it comes.

She felt the statue squirm and twist under her hands as if it wanted to follow the rotation inside it, then something gave way with a snap; the head of the securing pin shot out, with its length of chain. The Basilisk slewed on its pillar and Helen, wrenched round with it, saw the beam rake the chamber in a sweeping arc, dissolving all before it – then she was flung through the dazzling air and the world exploded into light.

The end (for now).

The Fate of the Stone will continue in
Part Three of the trilogy, to appear next year:
Beyond The Gate: the City of Desolation.